EssexWorks.
For a better quality of life

Please return this book on or before the date shown above. To renew go to www.essex.gov.uk/libraries, ring 0845 603 7628 or go to any Essex library.

Essex County Council

A TROPICAL AFFAIR

Kamuna Island was Shannon's home and passion – and now here was Dane Kincaid with his ambitious plans, threatening everything she loved. Of all the men Shannon could fall for. Why did it have to be Dane, the man set to destroy her home and livelihood in Coconut Bay?

A TROPICAL AFFAIR

A Tropical Affair

by

Ann Carroll

Magna Large Print Books
Long Preston, North Yorkshire,
BD23 4ND, England.

British Library Cataloguing in Publication Data.

Carroll, Ann
 A tropical affair.

 A catalogue record of this book is
 available from the British Library

 ISBN   978-0-7505-3658-5

First published in Great Britain in 2011 by DC Thomson

Copyright © Ann Carroll, 2011

Cover illustration © Judy Kennamer by arrangement with
Arcangel Images Ltd.

The moral right of the author has been asserted

Published in Large Print 2013 by arrangement with
Ann Evans

Magna Large Print is an imprint of Library Magna Books Ltd.

Printed and bound in Great Britain by
T.J. (International) Ltd., Cornwall, PL28 8RW

CHAPTER ONE

Shannon surfaced from the depths of the warm tropical water, sensing the turbulence and the unease of the shoals of colourful fish that swam all around her.

Her satchel crammed with oysters and shells that she'd plucked from the seabed was being dragged by the strong undercurrent. Gulping down air and treading water she looked across the shimmering ocean's surface for signs of what was causing the disturbance.

She heard it first – the drone of an outboard motor, and then she spotted it and felt her skin prickle. A motorised dinghy was bouncing across the waves, growling its way towards the white sandy shores of Coconut Bay.

Squinting against the sun's rays Shannon recognised the powerful boat with the name Kincade Construction emblazoned along the side in bold black lettering.

Her heart sank. So they were back. They hadn't given up on the idea of destroying the copra plantation to build their airstrip. Clearly the fight was to go on longer.

Looking out to the horizon, she shivered at the sight of the Kincade Construction ship anchored out in deeper water. It was an ominous, sinister shape ready to destroy her home and the livelihood of everyone here on Kamunda Island.

Well, that wasn't going to happen. They'd fought them off six months ago. They would do it again this time.

The dinghy powered by, oblivious to her presence in the water, and she seethed inwardly as she was tossed around like a cork in the turbulent wake. Her temper flared. Had they no consideration for anyone? Not for swimmers, not for the islanders – no consideration for anyone but themselves.

Determinedly, Shannon swam towards the strip of beach bleached white by the tropical sun, her gaze unwavering from the dinghy and its two occupants. The driver of the dinghy was Gus Banners, red haired, stocky and decidedly unpleasant. At least he had been after failing to persuade Gramps to sell the copra plantation when he was here last. She didn't recognise the other man at all.

Bronzed-skinned children ran to greet the newcomers as they hauled their dinghy onto the sands. Shannon pushed her limbs to the limit, anxious to reach the shore. Already they looked to be taking stock of the view that stretched before them, already intent on the destruction they had planned.

Her toes finally touched the sand of the shallows and she waded out, squeezing the water from her long blonde hair before towelling herself dry. Grabbing her cotton robe from where she'd left it on a rock she covered herself before marching determinedly towards the two men.

Gus Banners stood mopping his brow, dark patches of perspiration discolouring his shirt. The other, taller man looked coolly at ease in his lightweight trousers and open-necked shirt. But there was something about the tilt of his head, and the air of confidence around him that warned Shannon she could be in for an even bigger battle than before.

Neither of the men spotted her approaching. The taller, darker haired one stooped to speak to one of the children who pointed towards Gramps' bungalow. Shannon quickened her pace.

Her grandparents' bungalow was along the beach from hers. Most of the villagers' homes were dotted along the sandy shore, many with verandas festooned with potted plants and trailing flowers where folk relaxed at night, sitting out, under the stars.

And beyond was a backcloth of tall palm trees, the wood from which had built the islanders' homes. This forest of palm trees was their village's lifeblood – Gramps and Krissie's copra plantation.

Shannon's blood boiled to think that these Kincade Construction people were intent on destroying it in the name of progress. To rip up the trees, flatten the land and build an airstrip. Her heart ached at the very thought.

She lengthened her stride, the sand hot and gritty against the soles of her bare feet. Still neither man noticed her, too intent on surveying the area, deciding no doubt where to wield the axe first.

Well first and foremost they had to get past her. 'Good morning gentlemen,' she announced her presence as she stood, arms folded, chin tilted determinedly.

A look of sheer irritation flitted across Gus Banners' face and Shannon registered the flash of annoyance … but it was the taller man's gaze that caught her completely off guard. The deepest of blue eyes swept over her and she was immediately glad she'd pulled on her robe rather than face them in her skimpy bikini.

'Shannon Jardine,' Gus Banners said, trying and failing to appear delighted. 'How pleasant to see you again.'

'Mr Banners, holidaying are you?' Shannon said, meeting his unfriendly gaze with a cool smile. 'And I see you've brought a friend with you to enjoy our lovely island this time.'

'Ah! If only. Unfortunately we're here on business, again.' A smile crept over his flushed face like some professional card player about to play his trump card. 'You haven't met Mr Kincade, have you? No, of course not, he was working on another contract when we were last here. Shannon, meet Dane Kincade, our top man ... owner of Kincade Construction no less.'

'I see,' said Shannon, extending a hand and fixing his intense gaze with a look which she hoped was equally challenging.

'Shannon,' Dane Kincade murmured as his hand engulfed hers, his gaze continuing to sear through her, gauging no doubt whether she was a threat to his plans or not. His cool grip held her a fraction too long for comfort and she eased her hand free. Deliberately she directed her speech to Gus

Banners. 'I'm surprised to see you again. I thought we'd made it quite plain six months ago that we are not selling our plantation.'

'Everything has its price,' said Banners cynically.

'Not here on the island, I'm afraid.'

'Think not? Well, I have news for you...'

Dane Kincade cut in, a commanding and controlled edge to his voice that warned Shannon he wasn't used to being disobeyed. Gus instantly clamped his mouth shut. 'I can understand your reluctance for change Shannon. You can't get much closer to paradise than this.'

'I'm glad you appreciate that, Mr Kincade...'

'Call me Dane, won't you?' he said, smiling. It was a warm, open smile not at all like Gus Banners' counterfeit expression. None the less, she remained on her guard.

'Dane,' she relented, acutely aware that his tactics were vastly different from the sledge-hammering ones of his colleague. But aware too that behind the charming, slightly rugged and far too attractive exterior stood a man of ruthless determination.

'Shannon, I want you to know that this time we have a much better deal for the islanders,' Dane Kincade informed her, his voice melodic – hypnotic almost. 'I promise you it will be to everyone's advantage.'

'I don't see how destroying our livelihood can be to anyone's advantage except your own,' she stated, trying hard to remain calm and unruffled.

Dane didn't answer straight away. Instead he looked steadily at her, the intensity of his gaze unnerving. 'You're not a born and bred islander, are you, Shannon?'

'I consider it my home, if that's what you're implying.'

He seemed amused at her defensiveness. 'I wasn't implying anything. It's just that there can't be many born and bred islanders with such lovely corn-coloured hair and...' he paused, stooping slightly to gaze blatantly into her eyes. 'Beautiful sea-green eyes.'

His compliment was unsettling. She wasn't used to strangers being so downright flirty, particularly ones like him. Nevertheless she stood her ground. 'I've lived on Kamunda Island for four years. It's my grandfather's home and his wife Krissie's plantation. I happen to take after my mother regarding my appearance. It doesn't mean I'm not fiercely protective when it comes to the people I love.'

'I can see that,' he said, sounding sincere.

13

'And you're a partner in the copra plantation yourself I understand?'

'You've been doing your homework, Mr Kincade.'

'I like to know who I'm doing business with. And call me Dane, please.'

Shannon tilted her chin and smiled sweetly. 'But we won't be doing any business ... Dane. Unless you'd like to buy some island jewellery?' She opened the flap of her satchel, allowing him to glance at the shimmering array of shells she'd gathered that morning.

'Very pretty. I'd like to see the finished produce you make,' he remarked pleasantly, leaning closer to her so that he could see inside the satchel.

Catching a breath of his tangy fresh scent, and for a second breathing deeply, she drew back just as swiftly, annoyed with herself for being affected by the close proximity of a man who was here to wreck her life. She flipped her satchel shut and said brusquely, 'I'll sort out some jewellery for you to look at before you leave.'

'Plenty of time for that then,' Gus Banners chipped in. 'We're going to be here quite some time. Airfields aren't built overnight you know.'

'Airfields aren't going to be built here at all!' she retorted.

Gus Banners' flushed face broke into an unpleasant smile. 'Shall I tell her now, Dane?'

'Leave it Gus,' Dane answered curtly.

'Tell me what?'

'It's not important at this, stage,' Dane said, a frown forming across his forehead. He looked suddenly uncomfortable. 'I know we're hardly your guests but could we possibly get out of this heat and grab a cold drink?'

She had the distinct feeling that he was changing the subject; he didn't look hot and bothered in the least. He looked cool and controlled. But she could hardly let them stand out here and boil. 'Yes, of course. Follow me.'

She led them towards her own house, deciding to warn Gramps and Krissie they were back, rather than landing them straight on their doorstep. Krissie and Gramps had been quite upset at all the heavy-handed persuasion that Gus Banners had levied on them last time. Her grandparents weren't getting any younger; they didn't need massive upsets at their time of life. And although Krissie wasn't her true grand-

15

mother, she and Gramps had been together for more than twenty years and was the only grandmother Shannon had ever known.

Stepping up onto her veranda that was festooned with clay pots and woven baskets filled with leafy ferns and island flowers, she pushed open the slatted door and led them through to the cool of her home. Her sitting-room felt suddenly very small and crowded.

Dane glanced appreciatively around at the gaily patterned rugs and the handmade pottery and pictures. 'What an interesting room, it's very you,' he remarked, following her through to an even tinier kitchen leaving Gus Banners to flop down onto a bamboo-framed chair, mopping his brow.

'Thank you,' she replied, deciding to take his remark as a compliment, even if it wasn't meant as one. Reaching into her generator-powered refrigerator, she did her utmost not to brush against him. 'Would you like a beer or lemonade, or iced tea maybe?'

'Beer for me,' Gus Banners called out.

'Iced tea would be great if it's no trouble,' Dane said, admiring the handmade 3-D pictures made from shells and corals that hung from her walls. 'Did you make these?'

'Mostly...'

Gus Banners' voice drifted through again. 'You ought to have a beer Dane. They make it from locally grown hops; two glasses and you're absolutely anybody's.'

Dane caught her eye and smiled apologetically, melting the twinge of annoyance she felt at his colleague's rudeness. 'Iced tea sounds perfect.'

He had the most disarming smile, and no doubt knew it, Shannon thought, pouring the drinks. She was fiercely aware too that she was at a disadvantage in a bikini and robe with her wet hair clinging to her head like rats' tails. At the first opportunity, once both men were seated with their drinks, she disappeared into her bedroom, anxious to dress for battle.

Closing the door on them, she quickly changed into calf length trousers, vest top and open shirt. Checking her reflection in the mirror, she flinched. Her cheeks were far too flushed which she knew was the result of being in the company of Kincade Construction's top man. Irritated with herself for even caring how she looked, she coiled her hair into a twist and clipped it up. Then slipping her feet into sandals, she cast a final look into the mirror and returned to the sitting-room.

Gus Banners seemed to have made himself at home in her flowery cushioned chair, while Dane sat on the edge of his seat looking far too masculine for the dainty room. She could well imagine him lounging on a huge black leather sofa, sipping a martini in some luxurious apartment, while some glamorous woman waited on him hand and foot. Was he married she wondered, then dismissed the thought. It meant nothing to her either way.

Both men glanced up as she entered the room, and for the briefest second Shannon caught the look in Dane's eye. It startled her. It was a desolate look. One she didn't understand. It left her feeling anxious – but with no idea why.

'Please ... finish your drinks. I'll be back shortly. I'm going to find my grandparents and let them know you're here.' Stepping outside into the sunshine, she was aware of an uneasy sensation in the pit of her stomach.

She ran to Gramps and Krissie's bungalow a little way along the beach finding Krissie slicing red chillies into a bowl and singing softly to herself. Shannon hesitated for a moment, reluctant to impart the bad news. But Krissie turned and saw Shannon

18

standing there and her dark shining face broke into a smile. 'Hello baby, catch any big ones?'

'Bigger than you'd imagine Krissie,' Shannon said, sighing. 'They're back – Gus Banners and his boss Dane Kincade.'

The knife fell from Krissie's hands and clattered to the floor. 'Shannon honey, don't say that. It ain't funny.'

'I'm not joking Krissie, I wish I was,' said Shannon seeing the colour drain from the older woman's lips. She put an arm around her plump shoulders, alarmed to find her trembling.

Krissie's dark eyes were wide. 'Why'd they come back? What they got up their sleeves now?'

'Don't you worry Krissie, they can't make us sell. And once they see they're wasting their breath they'll leave us in peace again.'

'Does your grandpa know they're here?'

'Not yet. They're both over at my place at the moment. I'll go and fetch him, shall I?'

'I reckon you'd better babe,' Krissie said rinsing her hands 'He's over at the plantation. I'll meet you at your house in a few minutes. I just need to get my breath back. That's one nasty shock honey. I thought we'd seen the last of them.'

'Yes, so did I,' Shannon said, angry with the Kincade people who obviously thought they could play God with other people's lives.

Outside, Shannon cut through the little plot of cultivated garden rescued from the tropical undergrowth where she helped Krissie grow strawberries, sweet potatoes, peppers and all kinds of crops and herbs.

Beyond the garden she ran on into the jungle of palms. It was shadier here and she waved briefly to the young boys high up in the green foliage cutting down coconuts. Usually she would stop and chat, especially to Corey. She'd always marvelled at how the young men were so adept at harvesting the coconuts. They could climb the tall coconut palms in moments then skilfully slice the coconuts free, allowing them to fall to the ground where their partner would slice open the nut and scrape out the flesh to dry under the sun before crating it for export. In turn the oil would be pressed from the dried flesh to make margarine, soaps and cosmetics. It was a small but flourishing business and a way of life Shannon had come to love. Today, however, she had no time to stop and watch, she had too much on her mind and so she just called out a quick hello and hurried on.

She found her grandfather hammering nails into a wooden crate. Dressed in khaki baggy shorts and a vest, his torso was remarkably wiry and fit for a man in his late sixties. He glanced up and his leathery face broke into a crinkled smile. Seeing her expression his smile vanished.

Putting down his hammer he wiped his forehead with a cloth. 'Hello baby. Is everything okay? You're looking mighty troubled.'

'Oh, Gramps!' Shannon wailed. 'It's the Kincade people. They're back and they've brought their top man this time.'

For a second, Joey Jardine seemed to sway on his heels as if her news had knocked him sideways. 'They're back here, on the island?'

She just hated this, hated upsetting her grandparents. They were the only family she had and they meant the world to her. 'I've left them at my place. I didn't want them just marching in on you and Krissie.'

He wiped his hands on the cloth now, shaking his head. 'Why'd they keep pestering us? Why can't they take no for an answer?'

Shannon shook her head sadly. 'They just think that money is the answer to everything.'

'Well, we're not selling – and I shall tell them so,' Joey stated firmly.

'Want me to come with you?' Denny, the plantation foreman cut in. Dressed similarly in shorts and vest, Denny's powerful physique would be daunting to any un-welcome visitor.

Joey held up a hand. 'No, no. I can handle them.'

Shannon went to follow, but Denny called her back. 'Hold on girl. I ain't seen much of you in days.'

Anxious to go with her grandfather, she pulled a reluctant face. 'Sorry Denny, I've just been busy.'

'We gonna have some fun at Krissie's party at the weekend, yeah?'

'You bet!' she agreed, feeling guilty at being so brusque with him. Denny was Corey's older brother and a good friend – not exactly a boyfriend, a disastrous relationship back in England had put her off serious relationships for life. In her experi-ence men just couldn't be trusted. She'd been stupid enough to give her heart, her trust, her loyalty – everything in fact to Paul – only to have him betray her. For him to let her down when she most desperately needed him – when she was grieving for her parents. No, she would never make that mistake again. But right at this moment she needed to speak to her grandfather who was walking faster than was good for him.

'Gramps! Slow down!'

'Sorry babe.'

'I really don't understand why they want an airstrip anyway?' she said.

'It's because of the silver ore and minerals they discovered a little while back,' he said, striding on. 'They'll want to mine it. And as we're only accessible by one small shipping lane because of the reef, they'll need to come in and out by plane.'

'So why not build their airfield somewhere else? Why on our bit of land?'

'Too mountainous I expect honey,' he said shaking his greying head. 'Who knows?'

Shannon caught his arm, slowing him down. 'Gramps, they can't make us sell, can they?'

'Of course not,' he said, patting her hand. 'Only the Australian Government can make a compulsory purchase of our land. And Kincade Construction aren't Government, they're just a private enterprise. Now don't you fret, it'll be alright.'

And at that moment, Shannon naively believed it would.

CHAPTER TWO

Reaching her bungalow, Shannon followed her grandfather in. The two men stood up as they entered. Dane's hand went out to Gramps instantly, his expression warm and relaxed. That desolate look she thought she'd glimpsed earlier, now gone.

'Dane Kincade, owner of Kincade Construction,' he introduced himself, towering over Joey, making him look all of his sixty-eight years. 'I'm sorry to have dragged you away from your work.'

Joey was on his guard. 'Seems to me if you have your way there won't be any work for me, or anyone.'

'Actually no, that's not the case, Mr Jardine,' said Dane, the slight flick of his eyes in Shannon's direction indicating that she was included in this conversation too.

'So you're not trying to buy up my plantation so you can build your darn airstrip?' Gramps questioned, straightening his bony shoulders.

'Well, basically, that is the case,' Dane said

24

softly, not flinching from Joey's sharp utterance. 'But I hope you'll hear us out Mr Jardine. We have a very good offer. In fact, you and your family will never have to work again.'

'And what about the plantation workers?' Shannon interrupted. 'We employ more than twenty people. What about them? They'll be losing their jobs. You'll be destroying all their lives.'

Dane switched his attention to her and she caught the glint of anger in his eyes, as if she'd unjustly accused him of something. 'Shannon, I'm not in the business of throwing people out of work or destroying lives. The new airfield will offer new employment for the islanders. People's lives will be improved. True enough that lives will be changed, but whatever, we remove, we will rebuild or replace.'

'So you intend re-planting the trees, trees that have taken generations to grow? My, you are a miracle worker!'

A small smile tugged at the corner of his mouth. 'Unfortunately miracles do take longer. What I meant was, we will make sure all of your employees are found new employment.'

'What! In a silver mine?' Shannon cried,

outraged. 'You think any one of these men would want to swap their lives of fresh air to work down a mine?'

'No. I'm not talking about re-deployment to a silver mine,' he said slowly, as if speaking to a small child. 'There's going to be an airfield here which will need people to staff it, in a variety of different roles. You'll all be re-trained. It will actually create employment. And, we'll re-build any homes that have to come down...'

Shannon's heart sank. 'You're going to flatten our homes too!'

That desolate expression flashed back into his eyes. 'Unfortunately it would be a necessity. You can't live directly under the flight path. It would be far too noisy and dangerous.'

Shannon turned desperately to her grandfather. 'Gramps, can you believe this man? Can you believe what he wants to do to us?'

Joey patted her hand. 'Let's hear him out honey. After all, he has come quite some way to make his offer. Carry on Mr Kincade.'

'I'll come straight to the point Mr Jardine,' said Dane, his expression deadly serious. 'We are tripling the previous offer, which I think you'll agree is far in excess of what your business is actually worth.'

Shannon saw her grandfather sway. His hands clutched the back of a chair to steady himself. It was an amazing amount of money. But Shannon's blood boiled at the attitude of these people, believing they could buy anything – livelihoods, culture, a way of life.

'How can you possibly put a price on a lifetime's work?' she demanded.

'Difficult,' Dane agreed tilting his head, making out he really cared. 'But not impossible.'

He sounded so confident, so arrogant, that Shannon literally shook with suppressed anger. 'We're not all governed by money Mr Kincade.'

'Exactly,' agreed Joey, his voice equally tremulous. 'We take great pride in our copra plantation gentlemen. It's been in my wife's family for four generations, and I would like my granddaughter here to take over from us one day.'

Before Dane could speak, Krissie walked in. She had swapped her flowery apron for a neat blue dress and clipped her unruly greyish-black curls neatly under control. There was a guarded look on her face.

Gramps introduced her to Dane, and

27

informed her of the amount of money they had offered. Shannon wasn't surprised to see her stagger too, and was glad that Gramps was standing close by to steady her.

Krissie linked her husband's arm. 'That's one big chunk of money, Mr Kincade. Joey and I are gonna have to give this some careful thought...' she raised her hand as Shannon gasped. Surely Krissie wasn't actually going to consider selling. 'I say we talk about this over dinner tonight. That's what I came over for. You two gentlemen have had a long crossing from your big ship out there. It's only right you stay for a spot of dinner. Seven o'clock at our home, yes?'

'That's very kind,' said Dane, inclining, his head and smiling gently.

'Won't it be too dark to return to their ship, afterwards?' Shannon pointed out, still trembling inside with anger.

'If that's the case then we can offer them a bed for the night too,' Krissie said. 'We have a spare room for Mr Kincade, and one of the neighbours could put Mr Banners up I'm sure.'

'That's very kind, but we don't want to put you to any trouble,' Gus Banners said, trying to sound as gracious as his boss.

Shannon's eyes fluttered at the hypocrisy

of it all and she cried angrily, 'No, you just want to flatten our homes and our plantation!'

'Shannon, honey...' Gramps reached out to her, but Shannon had heard enough already.

'You'll have to excuse me. I've things to do.' She turned and dashed out of the house, amazed that Gramps and Krissie could take it all so calmly. These Kincade people were trying to destroy everything they had, and her grandparents were offering them a free meal and a bed for the night. It was just too much!

Once outside, she ran down the beach, the warm breeze freeing her hair from the clips that held it back. It blew wildly as she kicked off her sandals to run barefoot across the hot sand. She ran on until she came to a familiar secluded bay, a favourite spot of hers.

This tiny cove amongst the rocks was where she came when she needed to think. And over the last four years she had been here many times.

Now, she sat on a rock, her arms wrapped around her legs and her chin resting on her knees, staring out at the gently lapping ocean, listening to the melodic zinging of pebbles dancing along the shoreline.

The tragic death of both parents in that horrendous car crash had left her bereft four years ago when she was twenty-four. But if that wasn't bad enough, a few months later the man she was engaged to marry decided he couldn't handle the fact that she was grieving and dumped her for someone who could provide the fun he craved.

She'd had to get away, and the one place of solace was to follow in her grandfather's footsteps and run away to the far side of the world to Kamunda Island.

Years before, when Shannon was just a baby, her grandfather, a widower, had come here on holiday. He had met Krissie, fallen in love with her, the way of life and the island and never returned home.

Grieving and broken-hearted, Shannon had moved out here to be near the only family she had left. She had found peace, tranquillity, friendship and a wonderful way of life.

Gradually the gentle lapping of the waves against the rocks worked its magic. Slowly her temper dissolved as she realised her grandparents were hospitable people. It was in their nature to show kindness and generosity to visitors – even the Kincade crew. Krissie was letting them down gently. They had come a long way only to have their offer rejected again – another wasted journey. Knowing her grandparents as she did, they couldn't have behaved in any other way.

She almost felt embarrassed at not reacting with the same calm dignity as they had. Maybe she shouldn't have charged out like that. But it was done now.

'Penny for them.'

Shannon almost toppled off the rock at the sound of Dane Kincade's voice. Catching her breath, she cast him only the curtest of glances, any intentions of showing the calm dignity of her grandparents gone in a flash. He seated himself on a smooth rock close by and began picking up pebbles to cast them idly into the ocean. 'I'm sorry you're feeling so angry about all of this Shannon.'

'How do you expect me to feel?' she shot at him, wishing he wasn't so cool and collected about all of this – nor so – there was no denying it – so good looking, although she was furious at herself for being even slightly swayed by a man just because of his looks.

'Well, I was hoping you could see this in a rational way, I guess.'

'Rational!' she exploded. 'You want to destroy our way of life and flatten our homes, and I should be rational!'

Leaning towards her, locking her in his gaze, he said, 'This is a golden opportunity for your family – and your employees. You need to consider this offer. You need to think about your grandparents. They aren't getting any younger. This offer would give them a fantastic retirement.'

She dragged her gaze away and stared out across the turquoise-blue ocean that she loved so dearly and demanded, 'And what about those who aren't near retirement age?'

'As I said, new employment with the aircraft company. Times change Shannon, it's progress. Once the mining gets under-way across the other side of the island, it will bring real prosperity to all the people on Kamunda. Your family digging your heels in like this is holding back hundreds of other islanders from earning a good living.'

Her eyes blazed. 'Oh! So I'm being selfish now, am I?'

'Actually, yes,' he murmured. 'But it's understandable.'

She gasped at his audacity and jumped to her feet. 'You're unbelievable! I thought Gus Banners was bad enough, but you...'

He seemed oblivious to her anger, and threw another pebble into the sea. 'So what your grandfather said – it's true? You were intending taking over the plantation when they retire?'

'I will be taking over the plantation,' she stated defiantly. 'It's a thriving business. Not the multi-million pound corporation that Kincade Construction is, no doubt, but we earn an honest living making and exporting copra.'

'And you plan on spending your life here on Kamunda?'

He sounded ingenuous and Shannon shook her head in dismay at his attitude. 'Who wouldn't want to live in a tropical paradise? Here you can breathe, you can run and swim and fish. You can dive below the waves and explore the beautiful coral. You can watch the sun setting into the ocean and see it rise again over the mountains...' her voice trailed away as she realised he was looking at her with a look of sadness on his face. Almost as if he pitied her. 'Not the sort of life you're used to, I imagine,' she bristled.

He picked up a shell and studied it. His voice didn't hint at pity, more of wistfulness. 'No, it's not the sort of life I'm used to. But to be honest, I wouldn't mind swapping it for a while.'

'Perhaps you should,' Shannon challenged, her hopes rising. If she could make him see why this way of life was so special, maybe then he would go away and leave them to live in peace. 'You'd see then why we're so opposed to change – and destroying livelihoods.'

His eyes flinched like before when she'd accused him of destruction and the wistfulness gave way to a harsh chord in his voice. 'Destruction isn't my scene Shannon, despite what you think. Six months ago my company completed a university down in New Guinea and before that a bridge back at home.'

'And where's home?' she blurted out, instantly wishing she could retract her question. His private life was of no interest to her. No interest at all.

Nevertheless, he told her. 'Just outside Sidney.'

Deliberately, knowing it would rile him, she asked, 'And what did you have to flatten to make way for your university and your bridge?'

'Not a damn thing,' he growled, glowering at her. 'Shannon, you've got the wrong impression of me altogether.'

It was hard to out-stare him, but nevertheless, she faced him squarely. 'But you can't deny that you'll have to destroy the livelihood of our village before you can achieve your aims this time.'

'Not destroy Shannon,' he said almost wearily. 'Change. We change people's lives and usually for the better.'

He sounded so sincere, so confident, that Shannon tossed her head back angrily. 'You can't possibly know what's best for my family and friends. Here, they have something to show for a day's work. What possible job satisfaction can you get from counting aeroplanes in and out?'

'It's a vital job. It will mean work for people on the ether side of the island, mining the silver and the other minerals. It's vital for the economy of these islands all along the archipelago.'

'So build your airstrip over there,' Shannon argued.

'It's too mountainous. People have already reconnoitred the entire landscape. It has to be in this region.'

'Well that's just too bad!' She folded her arms defiantly, staring blindly into the distance.

'Yes it is,' he agreed quietly, too quietly.

She glanced briefly at him and saw that he was looking utterly downcast, defeated. Shannon felt no remorse. Failure was obviously a bitter pill for him to swallow. Well, he would just have to get over it.

She waited for him to say something, but a deep melancholy seemed to have settled over him. It disturbed her and she shuffled uneasily, wishing he would say something. In the end, it was her who spoke first.

Her tone was flippant. 'Well, there you go then. Nothing more to be said.'

He remained silent, staring broodily out to sea, to the Kincade Construction ship on the horizon.

Uneasily, Shannon murmured. 'I have to go. I've things to do…'

Still sitting on the rock, he glanced up at her as she went to walk away. Then he stood, drawing himself up to his full height until he stood gazing down on her, that same sadness in his eyes – in his whole demeanour. 'Of course you have. Sorry. I've taken up enough of your time.'

She hesitated, wondering for a second whether they should shake hands before parting, going their separate ways – Shannon, to the plantation and her jewellery making. Dane to his ship and distant shores.

But he didn't extend a hand. He turned his back on her and stared once more out to sea. Shannon stood awkwardly not sure what to do, or say. She knew she should just walk away – but to her dismay, she realised suddenly that she didn't want to walk away from him.

The thought struck her like a thunderbolt. This man who was all set to destroy her life and home, had somehow wheedled his way under her skin. Damn him! She didn't want this to be goodbye.

Stupidly, she blurted out, 'Krissie will be hurt if you don't stop for dinner after she invited you.'

He turned and gave her a small, sad smile. 'Seven o'clock, wasn't it?'

It felt like a reprieve. 'Yes, seven o'clock. Do you know which bungalow is theirs?'

'Yes, they pointed it out to me.'

She felt odd, light-headed, confused. This was madness. She ought to be assisting these two Kincade men to set sail in their dinghy – giving them an almighty push out into deeper waters. Instead, she found herself moving closer to Dane Kincade, breathing in his scent, realising she was being foolish and irrational – and storing up heartache...

A flicker of uncertainty glinted briefly in his eyes as he looked steadily at her. Then a slight movement towards her – a vague gesture of what? An embrace? An 'it's been nice knowing you, no hard feelings' kind of embrace? She couldn't tell.

She stood, feeling as if she were teetering on the edge of something way out of her depth. And if she stayed another second, she might fall helplessly into it. And so she turned abruptly away, somehow keeping her voice void of all emotion as she said, 'See you at seven then.'

She walked away without looking back.

For the rest of the day Shannon attempted to settle to opening oysters in the hope of finding some pearls so that she could finish the necklace she was making for Krissie's birthday. Finding three delicate seed pearls should have thrilled her, but for once her heart wasn't in it. She found her gaze constantly drifting off to the Kincade Construction ship on the horizon, half expecting to find it gone each time she looked.

There was nothing here for Dane Kincade to stay for. There would be no deal and while he intimated he would be at dinner, he had looked so bitterly disappointed, Shannon was positive he would just get back in his dinghy and head off back to his ship.

Throughout the afternoon, she listened for the sound of an outboard motor starting up.

So what if it did, she chided herself. That's what she wanted, wasn't it? She and her grandparents could celebrate the fact that they'd seen the Kincade crew off yet again.

She sat on her veranda, gazing blindly at the colourful shells, not really seeing their, sheen and opulence. In her head she was standing on the shore watching a yellow motorised dinghy head out into deep waters, her heart heavy and tears in her eyes.

'Stupid!' she muttered to herself, but nevertheless she got up and wandered down to where their dinghy had been dragged onto the shore. Seeing it still there, her heart gave a funny little lurch of relief. Surely if Dane was going to skip dinner, he would have gone by now. Which meant that he was staying for the meal – staying overnight.

He would still be here in the morning.

And for that, ridiculously, she was glad.

Strolling back to her bungalow, she spotted Denny and his little brother, Corey heading home from the plantation.

'Shannon!' Corey yelled, breaking into a run and launching himself at her for a hug.

'Hey, Corey! How's my best boy?' Shannon laughed, scooping him up and spinning him around.

'Good!' He laughed, planting his feet dizzily back on the ground. 'Hey, is Joey really gonna sell the plantation? Are we gonna have aeroplanes swooping in? Wow! I can't wait!'

'Corey! That's not going to happen,' Shannon exclaimed, frowning at him. 'Surely you wouldn't want that, would you?'

His bottom lip turned down as he shrugged. 'Dunno ... wouldn't mind.'

Denny draped his arm around Shannon's shoulders, an excited gleam in his eye. 'Shan babe, you heard how much they're offering?'

'Yes, a fortune, and they can keep it.'

'But you'd be rich, girl.'

Shannon shrugged his arm away and glared angrily at him. 'Denny! Gramps and Krissie have nurtured the plantation all these years. They couldn't bear to see it destroyed.'

'Shan, honey, they'd be happy doing anything so long as they were together. And think girl, they ain't getting no younger. You want them to work forever?'

He was beginning to sound like Dane Kincade and Shannon shook her head in disbelief 'I can't believe you're actually on their side.'

He stood with the sun glistening on dark shiny muscles 'Don't just turn your back on this offer girl. This chunk of cash is gonna set them up for the rest of their days. They could travel, see the world. Did you know that Krissie ain't never left this island in all her life?'

His words left her stunned. 'That's because she loves it so much here! I can't believe you're thinking like this Denny. It would be your job going too.'

'There'll be different work, good wages too,' he said swinging his little brother up onto his broad shoulders. 'That Kincade guy, he was telling us all about working for the airstrip. I reckon I'd look pretty nifty in my new uniform, too.'

'What! He's been talking to you all? Bribing you with his promises, behind Gramps' back?'

'Not behind your Gramps' back. Joey was right there listening.'

Shannon's heart plummeted. 'But he hasn't agreed to sell, has he?'

'No, he was just weighing up the pros and cons.'

Corey started to fidget up on Denny's shoulders. 'Den we going for some grub, I'm starving.'

'You're always starving.' Denny grinned, reaching up to tickle the boy, making him squirm even more. 'Come on then. I'll see you later Shan, and don't look so worried. Your Gramps is a smart guy. He knows exactly what he's doing.'

Shannon was desperate to talk to her grandfather, but not trusting herself to speak civilly to Dane Kincade should she happen to bump into him, she went back home and filled the time by getting ready for dinner.

She showered and washed her hair, letting the sun dry it. Then plaiting two strands at the front she twisted them around to secure at the back, leaving the rest to hang like strands of golden silk around her shoulders.

She dressed in a red silk kimono-style dress and while she rarely wore make-up, for once, as she was filling in time, she applied a hint of eye shadow and mascara and a sliver of pale pink lipstick.

The sand was cool as she walked towards her grandparents' home just before seven that evening. The sun was a massive ball of red, hanging low in the silvery sky, already casting its brilliance over the serene ocean.

For once, its magnificence was lost on her.

Her heart was pounding and there was a knot of nerves in her stomach. At this rate she wouldn't be able to stomach any food in Dane Kincade's company – that's if he turned up. She was beginning to hope he wouldn't.

But he was already there, looking refreshed. Gus Banners was spruced up too, and Shannon wondered why they'd brought a change of clothes with them. They had obviously expected to succeed in their bid and stay a day or so. They'd clearly struck lucky in getting a free meal thrown in too.

Gramps was in the process of pouring them drinks when she walked in.

Dane was first to his feet as she entered and his piercing blue eyes swept over her from head to toe and a smile came automatically to his lips. She barely returned it, avoiding his eyes to look directly at her grandfather.

Gramps gave her a hug. 'Here's my baby and doesn't she look an absolute treat? Gentlemen, is my granddaughter a beauty, or what?'

'Stunning,' Dane said softly, his eyes not leaving her for a second.

Gus Banners said something too, but Shannon barely heard it. Her ears were buzzing, her heart was thumping, and she honestly didn't know whether she was thrilled because Dane was here, in the same room as her, or furious because he was turning everyone's head about his wretched airstrip, making out it was a good thing to sell up.

She said nothing, but smiled at her grandfather, accepting the slender glass of the sweet amber liquid he handed her.

'This is pure nectar,' Gus Banners remarked, accepting a refill.

'It's made from locally grown kumquats,' Shannon said to no one in particular, but stressing the point that the island's produce was vital in everyday life. 'Excuse me, I'll see if Krissie needs a hand.'

The aromas in the kitchen were intoxicating – freshly baked bread, chicken and spices. Shannon's thoughts of being unable to eat miraculously vanished and her stomach rumbled, reminding her that she hadn't eaten at all today.

'Can you bring through the bread and butter babe?' Krissie asked, as she carried a tureen of soup through to the sitting-room. Beaming a smile to one and all she invited them to sit down at her table.

Shannon found herself seated directly opposite Dane, with Gus Banners to her right, Krissie opposite him and Gramps at the head of the table. She avoided Dane's eyes at all costs, even though there were times when it felt as if his gaze was burning into her like a laser beam.

Krissie ladled out piping hot spicy pumpkin soup, and the conversation remained on the subject of food which made for easy light-hearted banter.

To Shannon's surprise, she actually started to relax and enjoy the evening – and the company. Everyone seemed to be avoiding the subject of the airstrip which she guessed was just good table manners although she had no doubt the subject would raise its ugly head again before too long. Dane Kincade wasn't going to give up this easily, she was sure.

Not surprisingly, during the main course the conversation focused on what everyone's favourite food was.

Dane was clearly enjoying the dish Krissie had made for them. He dabbed his lips with a napkin. 'Well until I tasted that fantastic ginger and lime chicken which you've just served up Krissie, I'd have said my favourite meal was a thick, medium-rare steak when I'm ravenous and sushi for a special treat. But now I have to say that this is my favourite dish of all time. I'm going to have to ask you for the recipe.'

Krissie laughed. 'I think you're just being kind. It's nothing but grilled chicken with a few spices and lime juice. It ain't nothing special.'

'You're being too modest Krissie,' said Dane, glancing directly at Shannon from beneath his long dark eyelashes. 'I'd say this is very special.'

Shannon felt the heat rise inside her, and she fought down the sensation that she was about to blush. Frantically she reminded herself that he didn't mean she was special, as his glance implied. She took a gulp of water and warned herself to stop being so fanciful.

He was still looking at her, but this time more openly as he said, 'How about you Shannon, are you a steak girl or sushi girl?'

'I've never eaten sushi,' she admitted, unable to avoid his eyes any longer. They were the most vivid blue, as blue as the ocean and so deep she felt as if she were drowning in them. Aware suddenly that he was awaiting her reply she swiftly put a stop to any unlikely notions and forced herself to sound disinterested. 'It's never appealed to me.'

'You might be surprised. Japanese sushi chefs are apprenticed for many years learning the precise techniques.'

'No doubt, but you haven't tasted anything until you've eaten our local bonito caught off these shores, wrapped in palm leaves from the trees you want to tear down and baked over an open fire on the beach and eaten with your fingers under the stars.'

'That sounds wonderful,' Dane said, his eyes shining as they continued to gaze at her. 'I would love to experience that. Tomorrow perhaps?'

Ridiculously, she felt her heart leap although nothing showed in her face. Calmly she remarked, 'Won't you have left here by then?'

'How could I possibly leave after that beautiful description of the local fare?' he said, smiling broadly. Then his gaze switched to Joey and Krissie. 'Beach barbecue tomorrow?'

'I'm up for that,' Gus said, emptying his glass for the umpteenth time.

'Beach barbecues are for you young folk,' said Krissie, giving Shannon a sly wink. 'I'm sure Shannon will take good care of you Mr Kincade.'

Dane inclined his head, an eager, slightly

47

boyish expression that was totally captivating on his face. 'Will you Shannon?'

She knew she ought to decline, to say she had a prior engagement. But she couldn't. It was as if she was slowly and unavoidably becoming more and more entwined with Dane Kincade – a man who was all set to destroy her home, her life, her sanctuary – and maybe her heart too.

CHAPTER THREE

There was no talk about the airstrip until they had eaten the fresh fruit salad that Krissie had prepared and finished with coffee and brandy. The three men drank a glass of finest Cognac from Gramps' special bottle that usually only made an appearance at Christmas time and birthdays.

Shannon couldn't see any reason for celebration, but remained quiet, doing her best to adopt the dignified hospitality of her grandparents to these unwelcome guests.

It was as the men sat toying with brandy in huge glasses and Shannon was helping Krissie with the washing up that the conversation turned to the inevitable. She and Krissie could hear perfectly clearly through the thin walls what was being discussed.

Dane went over his offer again, going into fine detail about the changes that would be made, and the new lives awaiting them.

Although Shannon was loath to admit it, what Dane Kincade was offering made sense in a way. Mining the silver would bring prosperity to these islands. And Dane did truly sound as if he really believed in what he was hoping to achieve.

Finally, Shannon glanced at Krissie and murmured uneasily, 'He's very persuasive, isn't he?'

Krissie dried her hands. 'That he is honey. I think we got more important things to do right now than washing the dishes. You coming babe...?'

In the living room, Joey moved along the sofa to allow Krissie to sit beside him. Shannon remained standing by the door. Shaking his greying head, Joey sighed. 'Mr Kincade, you make it so difficult for me. I understand all that you've said. I can see the need to get the silver and minerals mined, I appreciate it's important to the island's economy. And I agree that it would surely bring the islanders the wealth that they so badly need. But to destroy the plantation...'

'We have tried to see your side of this matter,' Krissie added, taking her husband's hand. 'Now please, see our side of it. This is our home, our lives. It's all we have.'

'But you could have so much more,' Dane said forcefully. 'Once this deal is settled you'll have enough money to do whatever your heart desires. Even buy another piece of land and make copra again, if that's what you want.'

'Then why can't you build somewhere else?' Shannon begged, looking at Dane. 'Why have you chosen our piece of the island for your airstrip?'

Dane placed his brandy glass down on the little bamboo table and looked directly at Shannon. 'After you turned down my colleague Gus's offer six months ago, we sent a team over to look for another, suitable plot. They came back with nothing. It's either too mountainous or too swampy. I'm really sorry Shannon. There's no alternative.'

'Ah, but there is an alternative;' Gramps said, getting to his feet. 'This land is ours. It's not for sale and that's all there is to it. Gentlemen, the subject is now closed!'

Shannon's heart swelled with pride as Gramps stood up to these powerful men.

Krissie got up and stood beside him, threading her arm through his. 'Forgive us if we sound rude Mr Kincade, Mr Banners. But as my husband says, the land isn't for sale. However, we aren't pushing you out of our home. There's a bed here for you Mr Kincade, and our neighbours have a room ready for you Mr Banners. Only we don't wish to hear any more about your airfield.'

51

Gus Banners eased himself out of his chair, about to say something, but a swift glance from Dane sent him back into his seat, mouth clamped shut.

Instead Dane spoke. 'Allow me to say this. We appreciate your hospitality and I for one will be glad to accept your offer of a bed for the night. And starting tomorrow, Gus and I will do a tour of the island ourselves, and see if there's anywhere our team has overlooked.'

Joey nodded. 'That sounds like a mighty good idea considering you've come all this way.'

Krissie smiled. 'And our home is yours Mr Kincade, for as long as you need it.'

'Thank you,' Dane answered sincerely, without so much as a glance in Shannon's direction.

She was glad. She didn't want to give away the fact that the idea of him staying around a little longer without the threat of them trying to buy her land was a pleasant one. But if she stayed in the room a fraction longer, her inner happiness might just show on her face.

The following morning the plantation was buzzing with talk about the Kincade Construction offer, and Shannon had to quickly remind everyone that it wasn't going to happen. Joey Jardine had turned the offer down.

The amount of disappointed faces worried her.

By afternoon, she was starting to feel really annoyed with Dane Kincade and his wretched offer. It was like dangling a carrot in front of people's noses, letting them dream of some fantastic, wealthy existence.

Denny in particular seemed to have set his heart on a new career. She could hear him and Joey discussing the subject as they crated up more copra ready to export.

'We can't halt progress,' Denny was saying. 'Most of the islands along the archipelago have airfields now. It had to happen to Kamunda eventually.'

Dismayed by everyone's reaction, Shannon walked back to her bungalow, needing to get Krissie's necklace finished in time for her birthday on Saturday and determined to stop worrying about something that wasn't going to happen.

She worked all day. Diving for more oysters in the late afternoon's heat, polishing any pearls she found and then intricately drilling the hole for the wire before threading them into the pattern she was creating.

The sun had long since melted into the ocean and the magnificent red and golden rays had gone, leaving the sea a silvery grey when Shannon was reminded about the suggestion of a beach barbecue.

Almost on cue she caught sight of Dane Kincade and Gus Banners walking along the beach. As night was approaching, she looked at the two silhouettes against the silvery background. It was easy to recognise which was Dane. Tall, broad shouldered, the certain way he held his head, that powerful yet graceful gait. By comparison, Gus Banners, shorter and stockier, moved in a more rolling manner. Shannon saw him head off towards the neighbour's bungalow, casting a brief wave to his boss. Dane seemed to be headed towards her grandparents' bungalow, but veered off suddenly and made a bee-line towards her.

Shannon quickly managed to look away so that he didn't think she was watching him. She lowered her eyes, concentrating on her work under the lamplight. As she sensed him coming closer her heart quickened its pace and she knew the colour was rising in her cheeks.

Determinedly she kept her eyes lowered,

staring at the pearls, even when she sensed him leaning on the veranda railing directly in front of her. 'Any luck?' she asked without looking up.

He heaved a sigh, and when he spoke he sounded weary. 'Not yet. What we saw today was too mountainous.'

She glanced up then and saw that he did indeed look exhausted. Sweat had darkened his shirt, and beads of perspiration glistened on his bare arms and throat. 'Where did you go?'

He ran his fingers through his hair. Damp with sweat it had formed little tendrils of curls that flopped over his eyes and clung to the nape of his neck. She hid her smile. 'We walked into Upalo – is that how you pro-nounce it? The main village a mile or so inland.' She nodded and he continued. 'Then Gus and I hired a couple of motor-bikes and checked out the northern parts of the island for starters.'

Now she did smile. 'I can't imagine you on a motorbike.'

He looked steadily at her, his eyes full of warmth. 'You have a beautiful smile Shan-non ... that's the first time I've seen you smile and certainly the first one you've given to me.'

She lowered her gaze, unsure what to say, afraid he might see how his compliment had pleased her. She spoke softly. 'Well you haven't given me very much to smile about, have you?'

'I'd like to rectify that.'

She couldn't handle this. He was too arrogant, too sure of himself. She just couldn't handle his type – powerful, rich, confident, married for all she knew ... and with the ability to break her heart if she let him.

She breathed deeply, repairing the façade he was trying to break down and with a coldness that she really didn't mean, said, 'Jump into your dinghy and sail away then.'

His silence told her she had hit her mark, and as she stared blindly down at the string of pearls, she could have bitten her lip.

He seemed to rally, and she quickly realised that a flippant remark from her wasn't going to damage his ego. 'I wasn't actually thinking along those lines,' he said. 'I was thinking more about tonight.'

'Tonight?' she mused disinterestedly.

'The local bonito you were telling me about – wrapped in palm leaves, baked over an open fire, and eaten under the stars.'

He had recalled her words perfectly. She wasn't sure whether he was mocking her or not and so she shrugged as if it didn't matter either way. 'Well I haven't eaten much all day.'

'Me neither and I'm ravenous.' He stepped back from the veranda as if he'd just realised how sweaty he was. 'How about I take a shower, get changed and meet you back here in half an hour?'

'The shower is the important bit,' she said, and laughed.

He cast a boyish grin her way. 'You know what Shannon? You really do have the most beautiful smile.'

She decided to shower and change too. After all, she'd been in a plain smock top over her bikini for most of the day. She would have freshened up whether she was barbecuing on the beach with an incredibly good-looking man or not.

She chose an ankle-length blue chiffon dress. The empire line made it perfect for the balmy evening. She clipped a string of tiny shells that she'd made herself around her throat and another around her wrist. A tiny sprig of white blossoms in her hair and she was ready.

When the knock came to her door, there was no mistaking that flutter of excitement in her stomach. She frowned at her reflection in the mirror, reminding herself that this was no big deal. Dane Kincade was not going to get under her skin.

He stood in her doorway, illuminated in her lamplight against the inky blackness of the night. His hair was still damp – this time from his shower she presumed going by the clean, tangy scent of him and the crisp fresh cut of his shirt and trousers.

'You look lovely Shannon.'

'Thank you,' she replied, biting back the urge to say, so do you. Those tiny tendrils of curls were still in evidence, and she resisted the impulse to tease one straight and see it spring back against his skin. Instead, as she closed the door and stepped out onto the veranda she said, 'You look as if you've packed for the duration. I've seen three changes of clothes so far.'

He took her hand as they stepped down off the veranda onto the cool white sand and Shannon felt a warm tingle run up her arm at his touch. Releasing her the moment they were on the sand, she told herself she was glad. Holding hands under the moonlight wasn't on the agenda.

'I admit I chucked a few things in a hold-all,' Dane remarked. 'Krissie kindly ran the iron over this shirt I'm glad she did, looking at you.' His gaze swept over her, warmth and admiration shining from his eyes. 'You look absolutely beautiful.'

She grinned impishly. 'You won't make me change my mind by winning me over with compliments.'

'Am I winning you over?' he asked.

'No!' she replied, softening her answer with a smile.

'Should I try harder?'

'No!' she repeated and laughed.

Walking down to the shore, Shannon loved the feel of the warm breeze against her skin and the soft chiffon folding around her legs. Loved too the nearness of this man at her side. She risked a sideways glance at him, liking what she saw.

The smell of camp fires burning and fish baking made her stomach rumble. Out in the shallows men and boys stood knee deep, shining their torches into the water to attract the fish, spears raised.

Dane stopped, clearly intrigued. 'That's different.'

'It's an art,' she told him. 'Just watch...'

One by one, the men expertly speared their catch and brought fish after fish in for supper.

'I'm impressed,' said Dane. 'I think if I tried, I'd probably end up spearing my foot.'

Shannon giggled. 'Yes, I think you probably would!'

She led the way to one of the beach fires, and sat down with a small crowd of friends. Everyone seemed to know Dane, and Shannon was surprised by all the names he remembered. Denny was in charge of the cooking on this particular fire, with Corey helping one of the local girls, Su-lin by cleaning the fish and wrapping them in palm leaves.

'Shannon, hey girl, you're lookin' a treat tonight,' Denny called over to her, his expression clouding as he realised that she was there with Dane.

'Mr Kincade wanted to know what our bonito tasted like,' she called back, inching a little further away from Dane, so that their elbows didn't accidentally touch when either of them moved.

Dane didn't seem to notice. 'I've heard good things about this bonito and I must say, the mode of fishing is pretty interesting.'

'It's a traditional method,' Denny answered, carefully moving the packages of fish on the grill so they cooked evenly. 'We fish with nets for the market, but we like doin' it this way when there ain't no pressure to bring home a big catch.'

'I'm looking forward to tasting it,' Dane said, but his eyes, so clear and bright in the moonlight were focused on Shannon.

She felt for a moment as if she were sinking into those deep blue pools, and then her gaze drifted down to his mouth and she wondered for a second what it would feel like to have those lips touching hers...

'You want some bread Shan?'

She jumped as Corey pushed a plate of fresh bread under their noses.

'Oh! Yes! Yes please. Thank you Corey.'

'Fish is coming!' He grinned, heading back to the camp fire where Denny served cooked fish wrapped in charcoal-black leaves onto plates.

Shannon smiled awkwardly at Dane. 'I'm starving. Bet you are too. Ah! Here we are. Bonito!'

'I certainly am,' he agreed, a subdued look on his face. Then taking the proffered plate of food breathed in the aromas. 'It smells wonderful.'

'Wait until you taste it,' Shannon said eagerly, unwrapping the palm leaves, and blowing on her fingers as the heat seared through. 'Be careful though, it's hot.'

They ate in silence, except for murmurs of enjoyment and giggles as the oils dripped down their chins. There was plenty to eat, with salads and kumquat wine; it was a virtual feast.

'That was fantastic!' Dane acknowledged, finally refusing another helping of bonito.

'Didn't I tell you?' Shannon said, as she wiped her fingers on a napkin. Dane did likewise and then taking a clean corner, dabbed it against her lip. She smiled. 'It can get a bit messy though!'

'I think I'm in need of walking it all off,' Dane said, gathering up their used plates and napkins, and putting them into a bin. 'Do you feel like a stroll?'

'Yes, why not?' she shrugged agreeably, taking his hand as he helped her up from the sand. On her feet, he again released her, and they wound their way between the little groups of people and camp fires until only the deserted beach stretched before them and the shimmering silver ocean.

They walked in silence for a while, enjoying the fresh balmy breeze, listening to the shush and zing of pebbles playing in the shallows, with the sound of laughter and chatter fading slowly into the distance.

'So tell me,' Dane said, glancing at her.

'How long have you lived out here in this little corner of heaven?'

'About four years. I'm from Hampshire in England originally.'

'So what sent you running out here to hide away from the world?'

'I'm not hiding!' she retorted, frowning at such a suggestion. 'My life changed, I lost my parents, so there was nothing to keep me there.'

'I'm sorry to hear about your parents. What happened?'

'A car accident,' she uttered, her voice cracking slightly.

He squeezed her hand and then released it, adding, 'But you left your job, I'm assuming, and friends?'

'Yes, I uprooted totally,' Shannon replied, making light of the situation which had in fact broken her heart. 'I decided to follow in my grandad's footsteps. He was widowed many years ago. He met Krissie while he was on holiday here.'

They walked a little further and Shannon was just thinking he wasn't going to ask any more questions, when he said, 'So who was he then – the guy who finally tipped the scales?'

She uttered a bitter laugh. 'It's that

obvious, is it?'

'To me,' he said with a knowing glint in his eye. 'Who was he, fiancé, husband?'

'Fiancé.'

'What happened?'

'Oh, the same old story. He found someone much more exciting and – dumped me.'

'Was he insane?' Dane exclaimed, looking perfectly serious.

She shook her head. 'I was grieving; he got bored with me being so miserable and found someone who provided the fun he craved.'

'You're better off without him.'

'I know,' she murmured, changing the subject. 'So now you know all about me...'

'Oh, I doubt that,' he interrupted. 'But do carry on.'

She smiled. 'I was going to ask about your life. Do you have a normal home life, or are you sailing from one construction job to another – notice I said construction, rather than destruction.'

He laughed softly. It was a sound Shannon liked.

'Me? Married...'

Ridiculously, her heart plummeted. She tried to rally herself. What on earth did she expect? Handsome, rich, he was bound to have been snapped up by now.

'...cheated upon and divorced,' he continued. 'Present status, workaholic. It keeps me occupied.'

She was glad of the darkness of the evening. If he had glimpsed her changing expressions, she would have been mortified. But there was no denying that she was glad he was single. Not that she held out any hope that something could develop between them. There was no time. Once he realised there was no alternative site for his airfield, he would be gone.

She looked sadly, out to the horizon and her gaze settled on the black silhouette of his construction ship, lit up with rows of pale yellow lights from its windows and portholes. The sight of the vessel was a sharp reminder that Dane had initially come here to destroy the livelihoods of her family and friends, and that troubled her greatly.

But now, as Shannon gazed out at the ship, she realised that very soon it would be gone. And so would Dane.

And that thought troubled her even more.

CHAPTER FOUR

That night as Shannon lay in bed she could picture Dane's face each time she closed her eyes. His melodic voice, his laughter; the way he spoke her name – the gentle touch of his skin against hers.

There had been no kiss at the end of the evening. He had walked her back to her bungalow and hesitated long enough for her to have invited him in for a coffee – but she had deliberated too long, and he had smiled, thanked her for the enjoyable experience of the barbecued meal, and left.

She lay in bed, gazing at the filtered rays of moonlight that crept through the shuttered windows and imagined how it could have been.

With a muffled sigh, she turned her face into her pillow and tried to banish him from her thoughts. But it was a long time until sleep finally came.

There was no sign of Dane around the village or the plantation the next day, and she guessed he and Banners would be motorcycling to another spot on the island in the hope of finding a suitable area for their airstrip.

With Krissle's birthday celebrations rapidly approaching, Shannon went first to her grandparents' bungalow to check with Krissie as to what she needed from town. Together they sat down and made a list.

Armed with a wheeled shopping basket, Shannon set off for Upalo walking briskly, the wheels of the trolley bouncing and rattling over the rutted pathway, the light cotton dress she wore fluttering around her legs in the warm breeze.

It was a pleasant walk into town with each bend in the path revealing a different panoramic view of the ocean. The winding track was hedged with sweet-scented shrubs, giant banana plants and bauhinia trees with their delightful purple and white flowers. Shannon picked one of the orchid-like blossoms and threaded it through her hair as she walked.

Reaching Upalo, the contrast never failed to amaze and excite her. After her solitary walk where she'd only bumped into one or two locals – one walking and another on a bicycle, she was faced now with bustling crowds and commotion.

Being the only harbour town on Kamunda, it was alive with activity. The market was bursting with stalls, piled with fresh fruit, vegetables, nuts, herbs and spices. The main street lined with shops had stalls spilling out over the pavements displaying handicrafts, woven rugs, silks and pottery. The smells were pungent, the atmosphere electric.

She knew many of the townsfolk, but each time she stopped to chat to any of them, the conversation was about the new airstrip being constructed in Coconut Bay.

'It's not happening!' Shannon explained for the umpteenth time. 'We aren't selling. If the Kincade Construction people don't find another plot, there's not going to be an airfield.'

To her dismay, most of the locals seemed in favour of the airfield, and on a couple of occasions, she felt her temper flare and had to bite back the impulse to ask if they would be so keen if it was their houses and livelihood that had to be destroyed in the process.

She finished her shopping as soon as she could, and walked heatedly back, the trolley groaning under the weight of her purchases.

Doubts were creeping into her head, and while she tried to push them aside, she couldn't help but wonder about their decision not to sell. Was she being selfish?

That afternoon Shannon went diving again finding to her delight the most beautiful teardrop shaped baroque pearl. She spent the evening re-threading Krissie's necklace to include this rare gem, utterly enchanted with the finished result. She had made a slim wooden presentation box too, covered on the outside with tiny shells.

The fact that she hadn't seen Dane all day was playing heavily on her mind. Maybe this time, he had returned to his ship without her realising. It was much later that she spotted him, and ridiculously her heart leapt. He and Joey were strolling along the beach, talking. She hoped he might call by and say hello but eventually the two men disappeared into her grandparents' bungalow and Shannon made her way to bed, disappointed.

The next morning, Shannon sought her grandfather out eager to know whether or not the Kincade people had found another suitable piece of land, hoping that was what they were talking about last night.

'No. No luck honey,' Gramps said shaking his head as he spread coconut flesh out to dry under the sun. 'But I'll give the man his due. He's certainly exploring every possibility.'

'Do you know when they plan on leaving?' Shannon asked, hearing the tiny crack in her voice as she spoke.

Whether her grandfather noticed or not, he gave no indication 'Well it won't be until the day after Krissie's party at least. I've invited them to stay and celebrate with us.'

Somehow Shannon kept her expression void of emotion but deep inside her heart was soaring.

She saw nothing of Dane for the rest of that day either, and on the Saturday, she was at Krissie's house from early morning helping her to prepare foods for the evening's celebrations.

Most of the other women in the village were helping too, each preparing a selection of sweet and savoury dishes, and as the afternoon wore on, the party atmosphere grew. The men finished work at the plantation early, and set up trestles under the palm trees for the food. Denny had made a huge bowl of punch, and set up two special 'thrones' for Krissie and Joey beneath an archway threaded with vines and blossoms.

'That's lovely Denny,' Shannon said, admiring his craftsmanship as he put some finishing touches to his efforts.

His dark eyes gazed down on her. 'You look lovely.'

His compliment was unexpected, and she smiled, embarrassed. 'That's nice of you to say so Denny, but I've been slaving away preparing food all morning. I feel a mess!'

'You ain't no mess girl, you're a real beauty. But y'know what? I ain't seen much of you since those Kincade guys have been around...'

'Well I've just been doing my usual thing Denny. I've not seen much of Kincade or Banners myself actually.' Ridiculously, she felt as if she was covering up. As if Denny could read her mind and know that she'd done nothing but think about Dane for days.

'So we gonna have a few dances tonight, and have some fun?' he asked, swaying his arms and hips as if the music had already started. 'And I've made a wicked punch. You want a glass now?'

Laughing she backed off. 'No! I've still got work to do. You should see all the food we've got to finish preparing. I'll catch you later Denny!'

Wracked with guilt, Shannon dashed back into Krissie's bungalow. She liked Denny a lot. Normally she was content to hang around with him. But suddenly she knew that he wasn't the man she wanted to be with. It was insane because in a few days time Dane would be out of her life for good.

Her eyes fluttered shut in anguish as she realised that Dane Kincade had unwittingly destroyed something else – her belief that she would one day marry a nice man, such as Denny, settle down and be happy.

With a choking sense of despair, she realised suddenly, that unless that man was Dane Kincade, her dream was a long, long way away.

As the day wore on barbecues were lit, bunting and coloured lights were strung from tree to tree. Children had been busy making garlands of flowers and gradually mouth-watering dishes began to appear until the trestles were groaning under their weight. Crystallised fruits, delicious seafood dishes with shrimps, prawns, oysters, crab and lobster. Sliced meats and chicken, rice dishes and vibrant salads, all sorts of dips and sauces, mostly spiced with chillies and peppers.

With her work finished, Shannon listened to the steel band that was now in full swing, as she threaded a delicate white ginger blossom through her hair. Her dress was calf length – the palest of peach layered chiffon. Strappy gold sandals completed her attire.

Walking back to Krissie and Gramps' bungalow, with the boxed necklace that she had lovingly been working on for months, Shannon couldn't help but glance around to see if she could catch a glimpse of Dane. But there was no sign of the man. Banishing him from her thoughts, she went inside.

'Krissie, you look fantastic!' Shannon greeted the older woman. 'Gramps is going to fall head over heels again when he sees you.'

Krissie flounced across the kitchen in her bright floral print dress with its flared skirt. She twirled and laughed, already in party spirits.

Shannon held out the slender box. 'Happy birthday Krissie.'

'Ah, honey, you didn't need to go to no trouble.'

'It's not every day you're sixty five... I hope you like it.'

Carefully, Krissie lifted the lid and her large dark eyes widened, and then misted with tears. 'It's beautiful! Babe, you shouldn't have gone to so much trouble for me.'

She took the necklace from its box and gasped as they both saw how it shone. 'Oh my! This is stunning. Honey, just think what you could get for this in town!'

'I didn't make it to sell.' Shannon laughed. 'It's for you because you're very special, and I love you. Here, let me put it on for you.'

They stood in front of the mirror and Krissie held up her thick curls as Shannon clipped the pearl necklace around the older woman's throat.

'It must have taken you an age honey, it's perfect,' she said, smiling.

Shannon kissed her cheek. 'Happy birthday Krissie, you deserve it.'

Krissie began to sniff quietly. 'The Lord knew what he was doing when he gave me your Grandpa, he gave me the granddaughter – the daughter I never had – too.'

Shannon felt her own tears begin to prick the back of her eyes. She blinked them away the best she could. 'Krissie, you and Gramps have been wonderful to me, since my parents died...'

'Here, here, what's all this weeping?' Gramps exclaimed, coming in from outside. 'I thought birthdays were happy occasions.'

'We are happy,' Krissie answered, a tear trickling down her cheek.

It was such a contradiction that they all collapsed into wails of laughter, until finally, damp-eyed, Shannon gently pushed Krissie into Gramps' arms. 'Here! Go on and enjoy your party!'

Joey threaded Krissie's arm through his 'Have you seen all that food? There's enough to feed an army.'

'It's because we all love you,' Shannon said, squeezing their hands. 'Now come on, let's go and enjoy ourselves!'

The entire village had turned out for the occasion along with lots of friends from Upalo too. As Krissie and Joey emerged from her house, the crowd parted, forming a pathway for them to walk towards their 'thrones' of honour. At the same moment, the steel band struck up the tune *Happy Birthday to You* and everyone joined in singing.

Shannon stood back, watching as Krissie was surrounded by well wishers and smothered in hugs, kisses and gifts.

'I didn't know what to get her,' came a voice from just behind her.

The sound of Dane's voice sent her heart pounding. She whirled round finding him

standing there looking breathtakingly handsome in a freshly laundered pale blue shirt
and slacks, his hair gleaming, his com-
plexion slightly more tanned from recent
days under the tropical sun. Somehow she
kept her tone casual.

'You didn't need to get her anything, she
won't expect a present.'

'She's been so kind...' his voice trailed away
as if something was deeply troubling him.

Shannon frowned, recognising that look.
She had seen it before on a couple of
occasions and it worried her. 'Yes well that's
the kind of person she is, kind, hospitable.'

He gazed over her head to the party commotion where Krissie's laughter could be
heard even though she seemed to have
drowned in a sea of people. 'Sometimes, this
job...' he uttered, turning away. Without another word he walked in the opposite
direction.

'What?' Shannon asked, running after him,
falling into step beside him. 'What about
your job?'

'Normally, I love it,' he said, sounding dis-
enchanted. 'I love the planning, the dream
of what we're trying to achieve. I love getting the workforce underway, seeing the
construction – brick upon brick, nut and

76

bolt after nut and bolt. I love seeing it grow, seeing a dream become reality. I love every, step of the process...'

'Until someone gets in your way,' Shannon said, feeling his passion and understanding his disappointment. 'A tiny cog in the wheel, someone like us, stopping that dream. Standing in the way of your progress.'

He glanced briefly at her and then looked away, as if looking at her troubled him. 'There are always obstacles. Every contract has its obstacles. You get round them, one way or another. But...'

His voice trailed away and they walked in silence. Glancing sideways at him, Shannon saw by the creases over his eyes that he was wrestling with the problem.

'Still no luck with finding an alternative site?' she ventured.

'I've one last place to look at, on the north-west side of the island.' He stopped and looked steadily at her. 'Come with me to-morrow Shannon, we'll look at it together.'

His offer surprised her – thrilled her. Blanking all emotion from her expression she asked 'Won't Gus Banners object to me tagging along?'

'No, Banners won't be coming. He's got things to attend to here.'

Shannon had the feeling that those things would be preparing for them to return to the ship. But determined to look on the bright side, she added, 'Does this one last place look promising?'

'To be honest Shannon, not really. Remember, my team have already looked all over Kamunda, hence the reason for our offer to you. But we'll take another look.'

She saw not a glimmer of hope in his eyes. 'And what happens if this proves unsuitable too? What will you do then?'

He stood, looking back at the party, and the bungalows dotted along the beach, and the stretch of coconut palms that stood in his way. Finally, his gaze shifted back to Shannon, and his eyes held hers with a look that seared her soul. Softly he said, 'I don't know.'

She felt ridiculously sorry for standing in his way, standing in the way of progress. And the faces and words of practically everyone she'd spoken to about the airstrip came tumbling back through her mind. 'Dane, I know we're probably being totally selfish, but...'

He silenced her by softly placing a finger against her lips. The sensation sent tingles down her spine.

'I understand – totally.'

She went to speak again, but to her amazement, he took her hand, leading her towards the party.

'Let's enjoy the evening, shall we?'

As ever, he released her hand at the first opportunity, but still, Shannon felt ridiculously happy. Tonight she was with Dane. Tomorrow they would spend the day together. After that, only fate would tell.

The food was sumptuous and they were spoilt for choice as they meandered between the trestles, tasting, sampling, piling more onto their plates than they could ever hope of eating.

Denny's fruit punch was potent and delicious, and the first sip warned her not to be too over-indulgent. The last thing she wanted was to become tipsy and end up letting her feelings show.

'Be careful of the dips,' Shannon warned Dane as they found a couple of chairs to relax in. 'They go a bit overboard on the hot and spicy sometimes.'

'They're fantastic,' Dane said, smiling warmly at her, the anxiety of earlier now gone, or at least pushed to the back of his mind. 'Have you tasted this chicken?'

She peered at his plate. 'Oh, I didn't have

room for any of that. It looks gorgeous, though.'

'It's out of this world – try a piece.'

He held a small morsel up to her lips, and as she took it, his thumb brushed her lower lip in a way she found totally erotic. She ate, keeping her eyes lowered, knowing he was looking at her.

'Lovely,' she nodded.

'Do you miss home?' he asked, startling her with his sudden question.

She cast him a bemused smile. 'I am home.'

'Your former home. England, Hampshire – your job, your friends, the English weather?'

She was about to dismiss his question out of hand, but she hesitated. She missed her parents and the friends she used to know. She missed the countryside in autumn, and Christmas trees and carol singers and snow. Softly she admitted, 'Yes, there are some things I miss.'

'Such as?'

'My parents.'

He nodded his dark head. 'Understandable. What else?'

Images were forming in her mind. 'The changing seasons, although I probably moaned like everyone else when it was cold and drizzling or we'd had a sprinkling of snow and it had turned to slush.'

He smiled. 'What was your job back then?'

'Fitness instructor. I worked at the local leisure centre. I taught swimming and life saving too. A bit of everything really. It was fun.'

'That explains the perfect figure,' he said, blatantly casting a roving eye over her body.

It was meant to tease and she laughed at his audacity. 'Thank you. The swimming does help.'

'But do you miss him? The guy who finally pushed you over the edge?'

Shannon looked steadily at him, noting the hard angular lines of his face, the long black lashes that framed those deep blue eyes that were now glinting with curiosity. 'That's not how I would phrase it, but no, I don't miss him at all.' Turning the tables, she asked flippantly, 'How about you? Mr Married, cheated on and divorced. Did she break your heart?'

It was his turn to glance away, and he gazed off into the distance watching the party-goers for so long, Shannon was beginning to think she had hit a raw nerve.

'At the time I thought she had,' Dane finally admitted, as if he'd really had to think hard before answering. He levelled his blue eyes directly at Shannon and added, 'But in truth, I don't think she even scratched the surface.'

Shannon frowned, unsure what to make of his response and she floundered for some kind of reply. In fact he gave her no time to think, as he suddenly put their plates aside, took her hand and brought her to her feet.

'Time to dance off some of this fine fare,' he suggested threading her arm through his. 'Shall we?'

'Delighted!' she acknowledged with the same pomposity and adding a little curtsy. Then, smiling happily she allowed herself to be led back into the throes of the festivities and dancers where Dane's hand cupped the small of her back, his other hand holding hers, and he twirled her madly, until she was giddy and laughing.

The next song was a slower tempo, and he slid both hands around her back, inviting her to rest her hands on his shoulders. Shannon gazed up into his face, loving the curve of his lips, the intensity of his eyes gazing down into hers. Never had there felt a better place to be than in this man's arms.

But she jumped suddenly, the magic broken as Denny cut in between them.

Grinning. 'There you are girl, I've been looking for you everywhere.'

'Ah! My fault,' Dane said, his arms springing open like Denny had just hit a release button. 'I've been monopolising her for far too long.'

Shannon's throat tightened. She didn't want Dane to release her, and she certainly didn't welcome Denny's arm around her waist or being dragged away to another spot on the dance floor. But she pasted on a smile, knowing there was nothing she could do without making a fool of herself.

As she and Denny danced, she saw that Dane was standing watching her, gauging no doubt whether she and Denny were an item. Denny saw it too, and whether he was making a point or not, he took it upon himself to hold her tighter, drawing her closer and stealing an unwelcome kiss.

'Denny!' Shannon uttered, pushing against his chest. 'Cool it, will you. I think that punch has gone to your head.'

He stopped dancing, and stood there as everyone around them moved in time with the music, jostling and laughing. 'I ain't had no punch yet Shan, I got a real clear head. And it's as clear as day who your heart is yearning for now girl.'

'Just because I didn't want you to kiss me implies I'm in ... interested in someone else, does it?' she asked hotly.

Denny spread his arms innocently. 'It's okay girl, I ain't being judgemental. I've always known you and me would only be friends. If it was gonna happen between us it would have happened by now.'

She felt wretched. 'Denny... I...'

'You go to him girl, I'm sorry I stepped in like that. Go on!'

'I'm not going to desert you in the middle of the dance floor.'

'Dance beach,' he corrected her with a grin, showing he wasn't bearing a grudge. 'Anyway, Su-Lin is over there, looking like she needs livening up. I'll go drag her onto the dance floor.'

'Dance beach,' she reminded him, reaching up to kiss his cheek before making her escape.

Wriggling her way through the gyrating bodies, she finally emerged into a clearing. Those not dancing were sitting around in couples and small groups, eating, drinking, chatting, having fun.

Shannon stood for a moment, looking round, looking for Dane. There was no sign of him amongst any of the little bands of

people, no sign of him even with Gus
Banners and the crowd that had gathered
around him. No sign of Dane with Krissie
and Gramps.

With a sinking heart Shannon realised that
Dane had gone.

CHAPTER FIVE

Somehow Shannon got through the rest of the night, her smile locked in place and laughter on her lips. But deep down inside she was grieving.

When people started to drift off home, Shannon made her excuses to her grandparents, claiming tiredness and a slight headache – which was true enough, and walked back to her bungalow.

Crazily, she hoped he would be there, sitting on her veranda waiting for her, like an outraged husband waiting for his errant wife to return.

How she wished that was the case. But in fact her veranda was deserted, her rooms silent, her bed empty.

Amazingly she slept soundly and dreamlessly and was awoken at a ridiculously early hour by someone knocking on her door.

She stumbled from her bed, pulling on a short robe, half expecting to find an inebriated neighbour trying to find his way home. Her knees almost buckled when she saw Dane standing there.

'Oh!' was all she could muster. She quickly ran her fingers through her wild hair.

'Good morning,' he said, looking beyond her towards the bedroom. 'If I'm intruding I'll leave you to it, but we did agree to head over to look at that piece of land today.'

Shannon glanced over her shoulder, puzzled. And then the penny dropped. 'Oh! You think I've got someone here, with me?'

'It's none of my business,' he said, raising his hands and backing off.

'You're right. It is none of your business, but for the record, I slept alone,' she told him, her eyes glittering. 'Did you?'

His eyebrows shot up. 'Me?'

'Well you disappeared rather swiftly last night,' she said, realising she was shaking inside. 'I assumed something much more interesting had cropped up.'

'Oh, you noticed I didn't hang around then?' he asked, sounding genuinely amazed.

Shannon spotted the dark shadows under his eyes but felt too annoyed to worry that he'd had a sleepless night. 'Obviously I noticed! One minute we were enjoying the party, getting ... getting to know one another. The next minute you'd vanished into the night.'

He leaned against the door frame, head to one side. 'You looked otherwise engaged – you and your boyfriend. When I saw you kissing I realised I'd probably been stepping on his toes.'

'Denny is not my boyfriend,' Shannon said, keen to put the record straight, and stunned to think he'd left the party just because she'd been monopolised by someone else. 'Denny and I are good friends. He got a bit carried away, with the party spirit. That's why he kissed me.'

'I'm not blaming him,' Dane said, his expression mellowing. 'Who wouldn't want to kiss you?'

'Oh!' she murmured, the colour rising in her cheeks.

'Don't look so horrified. I'm not going to overstep the mark.'

'I'm not horrified,' Shannon said softly, her hopes soaring. 'I ... I'm flattered. I thought, when you just disappeared last night, that you weren't in the least bit interested in me. I thought maybe one of the other girls had whisked you away.'

'Let them try,' he said, a small smile curving his lips. Lips she so desperately wanted close to hers. 'If you want the truth, when I saw you and Denny together I was jealous.

It's not a feeling I've ever had to cope with before – not even with my ex wife.'

She could hardly believe her ears. Hardly dare let her hopes rise in the way they were rising now. 'You're teasing me – right?'

He shook his head. 'I'm telling you the truth Shannon. I don't know how you've managed to bewitch me in such a short time, but you've certainly reached parts other women have never reached – to coin a phrase!' he added with a wry smile.

'I don't know what to say,' she murmured, clutching her robe close, not daring to allow herself to believe what she was hearing. In a moment she would wake up and realise this was just a cruel dream.

'You could say, would you like a coffee Dane?'

'Would you like a coffee Dane?' she repeated, smiling, moving aside to allow him entrance. She closed the door behind him, her eyes not wavering from his tall, powerful physique as he filled her home with his presence, filled her heart with love. 'Sit down, I'll make the coffee. Do you like it black, white, sugar?'

'White, one sugar, please,' he said, relaxing in her bamboo chair, stretching out his long, muscular legs. He was wearing jeans and a black T-shirt; clearly he'd been back to Gramps' house to change.

She closed the kitchen door after her, needing to be on her own to get her thoughts in order. She splashed cold water on her face, deciding if this was a dream she needed to wake up before she descended any deeper into the realms of fantasy.

Filling the kettle, she pondered over his words. Could his feelings echo hers? Was it love, or just infatuation? She didn't know, couldn't know. It was too soon – yet what time did they have? Today could be Dane's last day here. That ship on the horizon couldn't stay idle for long. No doubt there was a workforce on board. He would have to return to them soon.

She made coffee for them both and took the mugs through to the sitting-room. Setting his down on the little table he smiled at her, melting her heart. 'I'll get dressed,' she said urgently.

'Wear something suitable for the back of a motorbike.'

She chose cut-off jeans, white T-shirt and trainers, and tied her hair back in a pony tail. Returning to her sitting room, and finding it empty, she followed the aroma of toast wafting from the kitchen. She stood in the doorway, thinking how tiny he made her kitchen look. 'So you can cook and ride a motorbike?'

'Er, not at the same time,' he joked 'Now I'm hoping you like poached eggs on toast.'

'Love them!'

'Good. So go and sit down. I'll bring them through when they're ready.'

'I'll get the plates out for you...' she began, making a move towards the high cupboard.

'I'll find them,' he said, ushering her out. 'No one is allowed in my kitchen when I'm cooking.'

'Your kitchen?' She laughed.

'At this moment, yes.'

'There's juice in the fr...'

'Out!' he teased, ushering her back through the door to the lounge.

Catching sight of herself in the mirror, she saw a smile that was beaming from ear to ear and knew that she had never in her life felt happier than she did at that moment.

Unable to sit still as she waited for breakfast, she took an embroidered white linen cloth and spread it over the table, then moved a small vase of flowers from the window-sill to set as a centrepiece.

A few minutes later he emerged from her kitchen, tea towel over his arm and a tray bearing steaming poached eggs on hot buttered toast. Two glasses of fruit juice completed the meal.

'This looks divine! Especially since I haven't had to cook it myself,' she exclaimed in delight.

'My pleasure,' he responded, sitting opposite her and placing her knife and fork wrapped in a napkin beside her plate.

The eggs were cooked perfectly and Shannon told him so, asking as an afterthought, 'Do you do a lot of cooking?'

'Eggs in any number of ways,' he told her. 'Steak, roast chicken, the basics really – as a matter of necessity. If you want to eat, you need to learn how to cook.'

'So you're not eating out every night?' she suggested, wondering if he would sense the note of interrogation.

He didn't seem to mind her question and explained willingly. 'There's a lot of business meetings which I have to attend in my line of work, and I always think business goes better when there's an element of pleasure to it. So discussions over dinner with a nice bottle of wine are often how my evenings pan out. But otherwise, left to my own devices, I'll cook up something simple like a steak.'

Shannon enjoyed listening to him. She loved the melodic tone of his voice, loved the animated expression on his face as he talked. She drank in the sight of him. Sitting opposite him over breakfast made Shannon realise that she could happily do this every day for the rest of her life.

'I'll wash the dishes,' he announced when they had finished. 'Then we'd better make a start. It will take a good two hours to get over to the far side of the island.'

Shannon jumped up. 'No! I'll wash up, you cooked. It's only fair.'

But he was already on his feet. 'Finish your juice. These won't take me five minutes.'

She sat back down again deciding that if this was a dream she definitely never wanted to wake up.

They set off walking into Upalo first where their rented motorbike awaited them. The prospect thrilled Shannon and she could barely conceal her excitement for the ride ahead.

'So you've never ridden pillion, Shannon?' Dane asked.

'Never!' she declared. 'You have to lean with the rider though, I know that much.'

He chuckled. 'We won't be going that fast.'

'I can't wait!'

Unlike in England, it wasn't the law that riders had to wear crash helmets, but Dane had arranged for them both to be kitted out with them. Standing beside the motorbike, he placed hers on her head. It felt awkward and ridiculously heavy. She fumbled to fasten the strap and finally gave in to Dane who adjusted it so that it didn't wobble.

With the helmet on her head, he stood back, gazed at her and smiled. 'I wish I had my camera! Hang on, my mobile phone!'

'Don't you dare!' She laughed, but too late he had snapped a picture of her and slipped the phone back into his pocket.

She was extremely glad she'd worn trousers as he straddled the bike and invited her to climb on behind him. She had no choice but to balance herself by holding onto his shoulders. Firm, strong shoulders which felt good beneath her hands.

'You okay?' he asked, turning his head as much as possible. 'If you get at all nervous give me a tap.'

'I'll be fine,' Shannon beamed, holding him tightly around his waist. She had the feeling that he said something as her arms slipped around his middle, but when she asked he just shook his head and revved the machine.

As they moved steadily forward, Shannon gave a little cry of delight and held on feverishly. She felt him laugh and relaxed her grip just a little.

Manoeuvring through the bustling streets was an achievement in itself, and Shannon marvelled at his skill in handling the bike and not bumping into any of the traders who seemed to treat the road like an extended pavement.

Once out of town they headed out onto the main road that circled the entire island. The wind was fresh in their faces and she was glad of the visor that shielded her eyes against the gust. Cruising along he turned his head and called out.

'You okay Shannon?'

'Fantastic!' she called back, and saw the corners of his eyes crinkle.

The views from the open road were magnificent, revealing the colours of the ocean with its crystal clear rock formations beneath the turquoise waters near to shore, then darkening to a dense inky blue telling of the greater depths beneath. Inland reared majestic mountains and deep ravines, and Shannon clung tighter to Dane as they rounded hairpin bends and rode perilously close to sheer drops of hundreds of feet.

But not for a second did she feel afraid.

After an hour or so of travelling, Dane slowed the bike right down, and took time to look at the scenery – or what they could see of it. After the ruggedness of the mountains and valleys, they had reached a long stretch of reasonably flat land but it was utterly dense with bamboo – masses and masses of impenetrable bamboo. Shannon knew instinctively that this was the area he was hoping would be suitable for his airfield. She knew too, that it wasn't.

Dane cruised to a stop and heaved the bike onto its stand. Shannon got off first, and was surprised at how wobbly her legs felt. He caught her elbow and steadied her. 'Feeling okay? Not too windswept?'

'That was exhilarating,' Shannon exclaimed, but knew this wasn't the time to rave on about the views and everything else she'd just experienced. Dane was already taking stock of the situation. And it was obvious what his conclusion was going to be.

He strode off towards the forest of bamboo, and for a while Shannon lost sight of him. When he re-appeared, his expression was grim.

'It's no good, is it?' Shannon said sadly,

when he finally returned to her.

He shook his head, his expression desolate.

She searched his face, afraid to ask what would happen now. Deep down she knew. He would have to leave. There was nothing to keep him here now.

He walked on, heading further along the coast as if he was hoping that the forest would become less dense. Shannon walked with him, glancing at him occasionally. The bamboo was totally impenetrable. It was a futile endeavour and she guessed he knew that too. She wondered if he was so disappointed and looked so despondent because he couldn't build his airstrip on Kamunda, or could it be because he would be leaving her...

She put that ridiculous thought aside. She couldn't allow herself to be fooled into thinking he had really fallen for her. But to her astonishment, he took her hand and brought it up to his lips. Shannon's breath locked in her throat as she gazed up into blue eyes. Eyes that seemed racked with pain.

'Shannon...'

She couldn't speak. She had seen that look on his face before. It told of some impossible problem that he was wrestling with.

His chest heaved. 'Shannon, I care about you ... I really care about you. It's slightly insane considering the length of time we've known each other, but meeting you has knocked me sideways.'

She was afraid to believe him. 'Really?' she breathed.

'Yes really,' he murmured turning her hand to kiss her palm 'You're the most beautiful, bewitching, feisty woman I've ever laid eyes on and I think I'm falling in love with you.'

Her heart soared, her head spun. 'Dane, I...'

'Shhh!' he whispered, placing a finger to her lips. 'Don't say a word my sweet. Just listen and remember... Shannon, I care very deeply about you and I would never intentionally hurt you.'

Her happiness plummeted. So this was goodbye. Perhaps later today, certainly to-morrow. Already she began to feel the pain that was to come. Suddenly tears pricked the back of her eyes. 'I'll remember,' she promised.

His arms went around her, holding her so close that she could hear the rhythm of his heart-beats. She coiled her arms around him, loving the feel of his body against hers, loving the scent of him, knowing she had to cherish this moment forever.

'Time we were heading back,' he said softly, breaking the spell.

His arm remained around her as they walked back to the parked motorbike. Wordlessly, he helped to adjust her helmet before preparing to set off. Shannon held on tightly around his waist, wondering how she was ever going to possibly live without this man in her life from now on.

The ride back was etched with sorrow. She clung to him, wanting to absorb his very soul, loving him as she had never loved a man before.

Too soon they reached Upalo. Dane returned the motorbike and helmets, and taking Shannon's hand they set off along the forest track towards Coconut Bay.

He was unusually silent, and Shannon knew he was deep in thought He must have such a lot on his mind. He would no doubt have to contact the people who had commissioned him to build an airstrip and give them the bad news. It would probably be a huge disruption to some mining company's plans. Without this contract maybe he would have to lay some of his workforce off.

'I'm sorry it hasn't worked out for you

Dane,' she said as they walked. 'I really am sorry.'

He uttered a harsh laugh that shocked her. 'Shannon, it's me who should be saying that, not you.'

She didn't really understand what he meant, unless he recognised the unhappiness she would be enduring once he had left, because while she hadn't admitted being in love with him, he must surely have sensed it from every move she'd made these last few hours.

Reaching the village, Dane seemed anxious to be gone. But first he stood and looked lovingly down at her, clasping her hands between his. 'I have some phone calls to make Shannon; I'm going to have to return to my ship.'

'You're leaving now?' she gasped, her heart feeling like it was being wrenched in two. 'So soon? Dane, no!'

His head went back as if she had dealt him some powerful blow. Then when he finally looked at her again, he gently said, 'I have to look at papers which are on board and there's a mass of things to sort out. I'll be back tomorrow. Gus Banners is staying put. I don't know where he is anyhow.'

The panic died down inside of her. If he

hadn't realised she loved him before, he certainly must know it now. 'Dane ... what will...'

He silenced her questions with a finger against her lips again. She desperately wanted to know what would become of them. Frantically she told herself that even if he had to sail away to some other job on the other side of the world, if he loved her as he'd said, there was still hope that they could be together. She was desperate to know whether there was any hope for them, or not.

Perhaps he didn't know. Perhaps he needed to get away from her to get his thoughts in order. Perhaps he was already regretting admitting how he felt for her.

'Walk with me down to the dinghy,' he said, holding her hand.

The sun was low in the sky, casting its golden hue across the ocean. The Kincade Construction ship looked so far out. 'Be careful, won't you. Don't capsize or anything.'

He smiled, as he hauled the vessel towards the water. 'You will remember what I said, won't you Shannon, that I would never deliberately hurt you.'

'I won't forget,' she said, vaguely puzzled.

He reached for her then, one arm snaking

around her waist, drawing her willingly to him. Lowering his head to her upturned face, his lips covered hers. It was a moment of searching, discovering, desiring, but a kiss that was so brief that when it ended, Shannon felt utterly bereft.

'We'll talk tomorrow Shannon,' he said, brusquely climbing into the dinghy. And then with just the briefest of waves, he powered the motor and roared away from the beach – and her.

CHAPTER SIX

Shannon stood on the shore and watched Dane until he was just a faint speck in the distance, and then he was lost in the sun's rays upon the water. She turned away, elated in one way, despairing in another.

Was there hope, she asked herself as she dawdled up the beach towards her bungalow? Yes, surely yes. They, were both single, and he said he was falling in love with her. And she had seen it in his eyes. Her heart soared...

The sight of Gus Banners heading purposefully towards her took some of the shine off her mood. She couldn't help wonder why he was grinning like the cat that got the cream.

'Shannon! So glad I've caught you.'

'Mr Banners,' she said warily, wondering if she should tell him that Dane had returned to the ship.

'I wanted to be the first to congratulate you,' he continued, still beaming.

'Congratulate me on what?'

He had been holding a document and now he waved it under her nose. 'On this!' he said. 'I wanted to congratulate you on becoming a very wealthy young woman – well your grandparents to be precise.'

An icy cold wind seemed to whip across the beach, freezing the blood in her veins. 'What is it?' she breathed. But deep down she knew. His expression told her.

He stopped waving the document about, and held it very steady for her to read. It all looked like a jumble of legal jargon, but what registered in her brain were the words 'Sale' and 'Agreement' and Krissie's and Gramps' signatures on the dotted line.

'I don't understand,' she uttered, a feeling of nausea sweeping over her.

'It's simple enough. You see, we had this compulsory purchase order for your land from the Australian Government all along. Only Dane, being Dane, does tend to take the long way round over these matters.' Gus Banners eyes swept over her in a way that left her feeling violated as he added, 'Dane says you can reap all sorts of benefits by not rushing things.'

Shannon's head was spinning, and through the haze, Dane's own words came back to taunt her. *I always think business goes better when there's an element of pleasure to it.*

She dragged the words out. 'You ... you had this purchase order all the time? Since you got here?'

'That's right sweetheart.'

'You never said.'

'The boss's instructions.'

She felt faint. She needed to hold on to something, needed to sit down. 'All this while you've had this? Dane knew he could claim our land at any time and there was nothing we could do to stop him?'

'That's the truth of the matter,' Banners said smugly. 'Sorry to spoil your day – you've been somewhere with the boss, haven't you? Yeah, he said he was taking you off for the day. Didn't want you around when the signing was being done, I bet.'

She felt as if she was going to be physically sick. No wonder Dane had disappeared back to his ship. He hadn't even the guts to stay around when she discovered the signing had been done.

She had been tricked. Well and truly tricked by the man she thought she loved. What a fool! What a complete and utter fool he had made of her.

She turned and fled, away from Banners' smug, self-satisfied face, sick to the very soul at Dane's betrayal and her stupidity in believing him.

Alone in her house, Shannon threw herself down on her bed and cried until she had no tears left to shed. She was a fool. Hadn't she sensed his ruthless determination the moment she met him? Hadn't she realised his methods of getting what he wanted were far smoother and more cunning that those of Gus Banners?

When her tears finally dried, the pain only grew worse. It sank down into her soul and filled every part of her with loathing and hatred and fury for Dane Kincade.

Gramps and Krissie came looking for her the following morning. They looked as red-eyed as she did as they sat down at her table – where she and Dane had sat only yesterday and she had been so deliriously happy and so full of hope...

'They beat us,' Shannon said miserably. 'They tricked us.'

'It was no trick,' Gramps said solemnly. 'It's all legal and binding.'

'But why didn't they tell us that from the start?' Shannon argued. 'Why let us go on hoping we could win?'

Krissie held her hand. 'Who knows baby,

who knows?'

Gramps got wearily to his feet. 'I'll go and tell everyone. They have a right to know.'

Shannon watched her grandfather go. He walked with his head low, stooped and broken. Everything he had strived for gone in the signing of their names.

Inside Shannon felt her anger burn. How could Dane do this to them? Accepting their hospitality, pretending to care for her, yet in the next breath snatching her family's land, home, livelihood – everything. How could he?

'I hate him,' she breathed, and Krissie began to cry.

News spread like wildfire, and to Shannon's dismay there was an air of rising excitement gathering. The general consensus seemed to be that this could be the change to their lives that they had been waiting for. Their disloyalty sickened her.

Denny had just stopped to talk to her when Shannon spotted a motorised dinghy heading into shore. Her heart turned over as she saw Dane at the helm and another four men alongside him. He'd brought reinforcements to protect him against her backlash. Her anger boiled as she pushed past Denny.

'He's not going to get away with this!'

'Hey Shan girl, there ain't no point in arguing with the boss man. He's just following government orders... Shan!'

She ran furiously across the white sands, a lump in her throat as she choked back the tears and the pain in her heart so acute that it could almost have been some physical injury she was suffering from, not just his betrayal.

She saw him bring the dinghy ashore, busily giving instructions to the other men. And then Gus Banners spoke to him. Shannon stood shaking, feeling as if her heart was breaking. Beneath the fury and anger the feelings of love were still there. She still wanted him.

Her knees felt as if they might buckle. Why did she still long to be in his arms? She was a traitor to herself.

Dane said something to Banners and then spotted her. For a second he stood motionless, staring at her, and then he strode towards her, his arms outstretched.

She ran to him – at him, stopping short at pummelling her fists against his chest. 'How could you! You tricked us. You lied to us.'

'I never lied Shannon...'

'You never told the truth!' she cried. 'And

I believed you were really looking for another site. I even felt sorry for you when yesterday didn't work out... Yesterday...' Her voice faltered.

He tried to hold her, but she thrust his arms away, aware that his crew were watching the whole scene, probably laughing. She could see Gus Banners' smug grin out of the corner of her eye.

'Shannon, I was looking for alternatives. I'd have given anything to have found a different site for the airfield. That's why I didn't land this compulsory order on you straight away.'

'No! You were making sure I didn't get in the way while your lapdog did the dirty work.'

'That's not how it was,' Dane stated coldly, his face paling. 'What I wanted was for your grandparents to have been happy with the offer we made. When they refused the last thing I wanted was to turn round and say well tough, because you've got no choice. So I went looking for an alternative site. It was a long shot, but anything would have been better than forcing you to sell.'

'But you have forced us!' Shannon cried. 'Only you've taken the cowardly way out, letting your henchman do the dirty side of things, while you went into hiding until it was all over.'

He looked mortified, but she had seen that look before and knew it meant nothing. 'I can understand how it must look Shannon, but it wasn't like that. Banners acted without my authority. My plan was to break the news to you today – you first Shannon, for obvious reasons.'

Her heart lurched at the tender gleam in his eyes as he looked at her, as if he was remembering the moments they had shared. She battled against any weakening in her resolve. 'What? Because I'm your biggest obstacle – or just the biggest fool...'

She turned, knowing the tears were about to fall, and she wasn't going to let this man see her cry. She would keep her dignity even though she had lost everything else to him.

She ran, her feet splashing in the shallows, oblivious to the pitying looks she was getting from the locals.

She didn't stop running, until she reached her little cove, the place she often went when she wanted to think. She wanted to black out her thoughts, she wanted to turn back the clock and keep Dane Kincade at a safe distance, where he couldn't hurt her. But it was too late.

Dipping behind the rocks in her own secluded bay, she slumped down and rested her head into her hands. Her heart was hammering and the tears which she'd held back, now came streaming down her face.

'Shannon...'

His voice, soft, caring, made her gasp. 'Go away!' she cried, frantically trying to stem the flow of tears with the back of her hand.

But instead he came and sat down beside her, his arm going around her shoulder. Furiously she shrugged it away and jumped to her feet. 'Don't you dare touch me! You're a liar and a trickster and a coward!'

'Shannon I'm sorry...'

'You're not sorry. You've got what you wanted,' she uttered, hating the despondent expression in his eyes. 'How you must have laughed at us every time we said we weren't selling.'

'That's the last thing I'd do,' he answered, looking up at her, misery etched in every line of his face 'It's breaking me up inside having to do this Shannon. If there's any way I could have avoided this, believe me I would have taken it.'

'I know a way,' she raged. 'Go tell your precious government that you won't do the job.'

111

He shook his head. 'Then another construction company will simply jump straight in and take over. And they might not be as considerate.'

'Considerate!' she mocked.

'Actually we are,' he said defensively. 'Rebuilding everyone's bungalow to each and every one of their specific requests isn't on the official agenda.'

'Well I hope you're not expecting me to thank you.'

'No, but I would like you to try and understand.'

She folded her arms, squeezing herself tightly as if that would ease the pain she felt. 'I understand all too well. You like mixing business with pleasure – you told me that yourself. And I was your bit of pleasure – a bit on the side to spice your working day up!'

He got angrily to his feet, but his anger was directed more at himself than her. 'That's how you see our relationship?'

'We haven't got a relationship,' she told him scathingly.

His shoulders slumped, making her feel as if she'd physically wounded him. She couldn't stand it, the way he was looking at her. As if this was hurting him more than it was hurting her.

'Anyway...' she said, holding her head high. 'I'm glad you're not laughing now Dane Kincade, because you've got nothing to laugh about.'

'I know that...'

'You may have a piece of paper saying the land is yours but that's a long way from having your precious airfield.'

His blue eyes became pinpoints. 'Meaning?'

'Just you wait and see,' she rallied, not really sure what she could do. But she was determined suddenly, that the plantation and their homes would not come down without a fight.

CHAPTER SEVEN

That night Shannon slept fitfully, dreaming of palm trees crashing to the ground and Dane standing there, laughing. She awoke in a daze to the sound of voices and commotion outside.

She stumbled to her window and looked out. To her horror an army of large motorised dinghies were making a bee-line from the Kincade ship to the shore, each dinghy carrying eight or nine men.

Panic welled up inside her and she threw on a shift dress and sandals and ran outside. Gramps and Krissie were standing on the shore watching the dinghies approach. Dane was there too, looking out to sea.

Breathlessly, Shannon clutched her grandfather's arm. 'Gramps, they aren't going to start clearing the plantation already, are they? They have to allow us time to harvest as many coconuts as we can.'

'I don't know honey,' Gramps answered bleakly.

'They can't! I won't let them!'

She stormed across the sands to where Dane was standing, waiting to meet his army of destroyers at the water's edge. 'Make them turn back,' she begged, looking desperately up into his hard blue eyes.

'I can't Shannon. I'm sorry. But if it's not us, it'll be some other company.' He took a step towards her, his fingers softly brushing her cheek, his voice hushed, 'But if it's any consolation I wish to God I'd never taken this contract.'

She jerked her head away, even though every part of her body longed to fall into his arms and believe what he was saying. She saw his eyes flinch as she moved out of his reach and his hand fell despondently to his side.

Her heart ached. She was trembling inside from that simple touch of his hand against her cheek and the look of pain that had shot across his face when she had pulled away.

But she was deluding herself. He didn't really care for her. Didn't Gus Banners say that Dane didn't believe in rushing things as you could reap all kinds of benefits by waiting? No doubt he thought she was one of them.

As the dinghies came up onto the beach, Shannon was horrified to see the amount of equipment they had brought with them – toolboxes, axes, chainsaws. The village came out in full force: men, women and children. The air of excitement broke her heart.

Gramps and Krissie turned away and walked back up the beach, arm in arm. Shannon ran after them.

'We can start again ... we can!'

Krissie shook her head as they carried on walking. 'Not your Gramps and me, we're too old. But you honey, you must find a new way of life. Perhaps the airfield will have good opportunities for young ones like you.'

'I'll never work there,' Shannon declared bitterly. 'I'd rather starve.'

'Don't say that honey,' Krissie said gently. 'This is progress. Don't let it make you bitter. An' we got something nice to look forward to. We're gonna go looking at a prime location for our new bungalow.'

'Dane said you're to come too, and choose the spot you want,' Gramps added. 'We're getting first choice.'

'And I suppose we're expected to be grateful,' Shannon said, her heart sinking even lower. 'Well I'm not coming.'

Gramps and Krissie left around midday with Dane and were gone a couple of hours.

Meanwhile she saw that the Kincade army had set up camp on the east side of the village just outside the plantation boundaries, erecting large green army style tents.

When someone knocked on her door later that afternoon, the last person she expected to see was Dane.

'May I come in?'

She turned away without a word, leaving the door open for him to enter. Her throat felt tight suddenly; she didn't trust herself to look at his face.

'Your grandparents have chosen a perfect spot about half a mile along the coast. It's quite high on the hillside looking out over the ocean. There's an easy path down to the beach and the scent from the flowers will knock you out. There's plenty of room for you to have a bungalow along there too. You'll love it Shannon.'

For the want of keeping her hands busy, she found a duster and began flicking it over her furniture. 'I won't be moving anywhere and I've no intention of being pushed around. This is my home and I'm not moving!'

'Shannon...' his arms reached for her but she turned her back. 'You can't stay in this house when the aircraft start coming in. We have to get everyone re-located and I want you to have the very best location. If you leave it too late...'

'This is my home. I'm happy here,' her voice trembled. 'Or rather, I was happy here.'

'I'm sorry,' he said, his voice so soft, that it was little more than a whisper. 'So very sorry.'

She didn't answer, and for a moment she sensed him move. For a moment she thought he might take her in his arms and she was ready to shrug him away even though it was what she wanted more than anything. But a moment later she heard her door open then close. The emptiness of her home matched the emptiness in her heart.

Over the next week there was so much activity Shannon hardly recognised Coconut Bay as the sleepy, tranquil bay she knew and loved. Dane Kincade's crew were everywhere and it was impossible to take a walk without bumping into one of them. They seemed to be very popular amongst the locals, especially the single girls, and most evenings the beach was alive with laughter and barbecues.

Shannon kept well away, positive Dane would be there, celebrating his success. Since the afternoon he'd called at her bungalow, she hadn't spoken to him.

As for the plantation, considering it was about to be cut down, it was a hive of activity, with, the workers making as much copra as possible.

After a week of intensive production the very last crate of copra was nailed up and sent into Upalo for shipment. Shannon stood beside her grandfather as the cart trundled away, feeling that her life was closing in on her. The end of the copra plantation. The end of an era.

Gramps stood with his shoulders stooped, the hammer hanging uselessly in his hand. He looked suddenly older than his sixty-eight years. A tired, beaten man.

'Let's get you home,' Shannon murmured, taking his hand.

He nodded, saying nothing, and at that moment, Shannon hated Dane Kincade more than anyone or anything in her whole life.

That evening Gramps and Krissie called by her bungalow. They looked strained and anxious and glanced continuously at each other as Shannon brought tea through for them all.

Gramps cleared his throat 'Honey, Krissie

119

and me, well we've been doing a lot of thinking and the truth is, we just don't want to be around to see the plantation cut down.'

'So we stand and fight them?' Shannon said, a glimmer of hope rising.

Gramps shook his head, as if the very thought was futile. Seeing his expression Shannon sank down into a chair – the same chair that Dane had sat in that first morning.

Krissie reached over and took her hand. 'Honey it would break our hearts if we had to watch them cutting down the trees after all these years.'

'I know,' Shannon murmured. 'That's what I've been saying. So what do we do? Maybe we can get a court order or something...'

'No babe, that's not what we're saying,' Gramps said gently. 'There's no fighting them. It's going to happen. Only Krissie and me ... well, we won't be around to watch. We're going to Fiji until it's all over.'

'What!' Shannon gasped, horrified that Dane was driving her grandparents away on top of everything else.

'Come with us honey,' Krissie begged, squeezing her hand. 'We'll come back when they've all gone and the island is ours again.'

Shannon sat stunned. In her heart she knew it was the sensible thing to do. To give in gracefully, to walk away and never see Dane Kincade again. Yet to do that, to never see him was too much to bear. Seeing him from a distance was better than not seeing him at all. Knowing he had betrayed her, tricked her, lied to her ought to have made her jump at the chance to get away. But it was as if her heart had been linked by invisible chains to him, and she couldn't drag herself away. She shook her head.

'We're going to worry ourselves to death over you staying put with all this upheaval going on,' Gramps said.

Her eyes fluttered shut. She didn't want them to worry about her. They had enough to think about. Taking a deep breath she looked steadily at them, a positive look plastered across her face. 'No, I need to stay here, to keep an eye on things. I'll be fine. When are you going?'

'The day after tomorrow,' Krissie said, and wrapped her arms around Shannon as all her resolve disintegrated and she broke down in tears.

That day came too soon. Gramps and Krissie had packed as if going away on a holiday and Shannon promised that she would ensure all their possessions were moved into their new home along the coast.

She stood with them at the harbour, looking up at the big cargo boat waiting to take them to the larger port of Bega and then on to Suva.

'Don't stay away too long,' she begged, holding back the tears.

'We'll be back before you know it,' Krissie promised, stroking Shannon's hair. 'You just make sure they build our new home facing east. I like to see the sun coming up in the morning.'

'I will.'

Gramps squeezed her hands. 'You will be alright honey, won't you?'

'Of course I will,' Shannon sniffed, trying her hardest to be strong.

'And promise me you won't stand in Dane Kincade's way,' Krissie said solemnly. 'It'll serve no purpose to antagonise the man.'

Shannon breathed deeply. 'I'll try not to.'

Gramps leathery face creased into a smile. 'Good! Well let's see you two make your peace now, then Krissie and I can set off with easy hearts.'

A rush of heat scorched through Shannon's veins. She could see her grandparents looking beyond her shoulder and knew Dane was approaching. She felt his nearness with every fibre of her being and she began to tremble. Suddenly he was standing next to her and her heart was pounding like it was about to explode.

'I wanted to catch you before you left,' Dane said, casting Shannon only the merest of glances. 'I wanted to wish you a good trip and ... and to hope you understand and believe my intentions about all this.'

'Mr Kincade, you've explained all that,' Gramps nodded.

But Dane went on. 'The last thing I wanted was to force you into selling. I honestly hoped you would come to that decision of your own accord.'

'Mr Kincade we understand,' Gramps reassured him, although Dane clearly thought he hadn't yet made his point.

'And on top of everything Gus Banners was not working on my instructions when he broke the news...'

Krissie patted his hand. 'We know all this. You've explained it a dozen times over.'

He stopped talking, heaved a sigh and looked steadily at Shannon, his eyes bleak. 'If only your granddaughter would believe me.'

'What I believe is irrelevant,' Shannon shrugged inching away from him, unable to cope with the tremors that were rocking her body at the merest touch of his skin against hers.

'It's not irrelevant. It matters a great deal!' Dane said, a slight quiver in his voice.

Shannon had no doubt that he was putting it on for effect. And clearly it had fooled her grandparents.

'Shannon?' Gramps said, raising one eyebrow. 'Will you two please shake hands so that Krissie and I can stop worrying? Please!'

Shannon saw the way her grandparents were looking at her. Somehow she pasted a smile on her face, extended her hand to Dane and said, 'Okay, I believe you.'

His hand closed around hers, his touch felt electric. Shannon tried desperately not to let him see how a simple handshake could rock her entire being and at the first opportunity she eased her hand free from his. The look in his eyes said he knew she didn't believe him at all. Yet it seemed to have placated Gramps and Krissie. They visibly relaxed.

'Thank goodness,' Krissie sighed as someone on board the boat began waving and calling for them to come aboard. 'Time for us to board. Take care honey. We'll miss you.'

Shannon hugged them both, keeping her smile firmly in place.

They both shook Dane's hand too, as if he had done them some great favour. Then walking up the boarding ramps, Gramps called back. 'Mr Kincade, take good care of our granddaughter, you hear me?'

'I hear you,' Dane called back, snaking his arm around her shoulder, and gripping her so that she couldn't shrug him off. 'I will. Enjoy Fiji.' Dane led her away from the harbour, holding her tightly, and only when they were well away from the boat did he say, 'Push me away now if you want.'

She did, but felt no satisfaction in doing so, only more bereft.

'Why won't you believe me Shannon? Do you honestly think I could behave so dreadfully?'

'Yes, I do,' she answered, striding out towards the track that led to Coconut Bay, needing the exalted effort to stop herself from crumbling. 'Gus Banner said...'

'I don't give a damn what Gus Banners said,' Dane snapped, his voice suddenly harsh. And taking her roughly by the shoulders he turned her to face him. 'Shannon, Banners acted without my consent, for whatever reason. Personally I think he was doing so to get at you. You fought him off six months ago; he didn't like that. I think he was out for revenge and he saw where he could take it.'

'So you're blaming him?'

'Yes! No...' he ran his fingers through his hair. 'Hell, no. It's my fault. I handled it all wrong.'

His grip on her shoulders relaxed, became more of a caress. He stroked her bare arms, sending unwelcome tingles throughout her body. 'Shannon, it's not too late to put all this behind us and start again.' His gaze softened. 'To take up where we left off.'

She could have melted into those deep blue eyes, they seemed to promise so much. How easy it would be to forget how he'd tricked her and fall into his arms. But somehow she kept her resolve and stared beyond him, into the distance. 'That's impossible.'

'Nothing's impossible,' he murmured, gently pulling her close. But she stood her ground. 'Please forgive me.'

She raised her gaze to his, knowing her eyes were hard and cold. 'How can you ask for forgiveness when you've no remorse?

You don't care how you're hurting me.'

'Don't care?' he threw back his head in a gesture of disbelief. 'Shannon, this is killing me. If I'd known how it was going to turn out I would never have taken this damn contract. Let some other poor devil see the tears in your eyes...' He stopped abruptly and turned away.

For one ridiculous moment Shannon felt that he was near to tears. And then she remembered who she was dealing with. A ruthless, determined man who stopped at nothing to achieve his aims. She stared at his back. His spine was set rigid as were his broad, powerful shoulders. The only softness was the sheen of his hair and the little tendrils that curled against the nape of his neck. Shannon fought down the desire to wrap her arms around his back and rest her cheek against his shoulder blade.

Angry at her pathetic weakness she folded her arms tightly across her chest, her voice little more than a whisper. 'But you don't care enough to give it all up? Pack up and leave.'

'Shannon, I'm responsible for my work-force.'

'We were responsible for our copra workers.'

'Someone else would come. The situation would be the same.'

She knew she shouldn't say this, she knew she was putting herself at an ever greater disadvantage. But what was the point in hiding it? Softly she uttered, 'Perhaps it wouldn't hurt so much if it was someone else.'

He turned then and to her horror his eyes were glistening. He looked at her, unashamed that she had moved him to tears. As she stared, she knew in her heart that it was the moment to take him in her arms, but some stupid ridiculous pride – and fear of being hurt all over again – kept her standing rigid. And the only move she made, when she finally breathed again, was to run. To run as far away from him as possible.

CHAPTER EIGHT

Activities around the village intensified over the next few weeks with the Kincade crew intent on building new bungalows along the coast for the locals who were losing their homes.

Shannon had no choice but to watch the progress. She had promised her grandparents that she would oversee their move, and with Denny's help and the help of some of the other local men, she did just that. Most days she spotted Dane but it was at a distance and not once did he look her way.

'When you gonna move your stuff into your new house?' Corey asked as she was rearranging all Krissie's dishes and pans into her new kitchen.

'I'm not moving Corey,' Shannon said stiffly.

'Yeah, you got to. Planes are gonna zoom in right over your roof. Me and Denny have seen the plans.'

'Have you now?' Shannon said, trying to smile.

He was unwrapping more crock pots from boxes, his little face deadly serious. 'You ain't even looked at your new place yet, have you, Shan?'

'I'm not interested in it Corey,' she said, as gently as she could.

'But you got a great place. It's gotta be the prettiest view, an' your bungalow is bigger than your old one. Me and Denny will help you bring your furniture and stuff over. We can do it today if you like.'

Shannon ruffled his hair. 'I'm busy today Corey. But thank you anyway.' It was her stock answer every time someone offered to help her move.

Four weeks to the day since Gramps and Krissie left, Shannon was awoken by a nerve jarring high pitched scream. She jumped out of bed and ran through to her kitchen window.

Everything looked normal. The view was of her vegetable garden and beyond it the forest of palm trees. Everything just as it always was.

And then the screaming stopped and another sound took its place – an awful creaking sound. Puzzled, she stood, nose pressed up at her window as the strangest sight unfolded itself. The palm tree fronds shifted. An entire treetop swayed – leant to one side. Someone shouted something. And then with a horrendous groan and crash, one of the trees toppled and crashed to the ground, sending up an almighty cloud of white sand and dust.

'No!' Shannon cried, racing from the house. Not stopping to put a dressing gown over her nightdress nor sandals on her feet.

The air was thick, she could taste the dust in her throat, feel the grit in her eyes. She quickly, spotted the culprit, one of Dane's men with a chainsaw. He and another man stood beside the felled tree, proud of their work.

Ducking beneath some yellow and black tape, Shannon flew at him, taking him completely by surprise. 'Stop this! Please, please don't do it.'

He staggered backwards unsteadily, holding her at bay with one arm, the chainsaw held at arm's length in the other hand. 'Hey! You shouldn't be in here. It's dangerous.'

Shannon frantically tried to plead with him, but suddenly she was being lifted bodily, strong arms around her waist, picking her off the ground and carrying her back beyond the striped tape, back into her garden. When she was finally set down, she saw who it was – Dane. His face was ashen.

'Are you insane, you could have been killed! My men have chainsaws. Trees are being felled. Didn't you see the tape and the notices to keep out?'

'Stop them Dane,' Shannon pleaded, tears streaming down her face, her fists clutching at his shirt. 'Stop them please.'

'I can't. You know I can't,' he uttered, his arms going around her again, this time in an embrace. And he held her against his chest, stroking her hair as she sobbed.

As the chainsaws started up again, Shannon groaned in misery and pushed herself away from him. She ran back into her house, slamming the door and throwing herself onto her bed. In desperation she pulled a pillow over her head in an effort to drown out the mechanical screams. The one redeeming thought as she sobbed was that at least Gramps and Krissie weren't here to witness the destruction of their plantation.

That first day only a handful of trees were felled. Then as the days marched on, the others met their same fate. The air was thick with dust.

After what seemed an eternity of commotion, Shannon awoke one morning to silence. She lay quite still, watching tiny particles of dust dancing in the bright rays of sunlight that streamed across her bedroom. For the first time in weeks, she could actually hear the ocean.

She rose slowly, hearing the floorboards creak beneath her feet, and then the swish of the hairbrush as she sat at the mirror. The reflection that stared back was red-eyed and pale. She dressed in a straight shift dress and sandals and went through to the kitchen. She had kept the shutters closed for days now, having seen enough dying trees to last her a lifetime.

She made breakfast but ate only half of it, expecting the peacefulness to be shattered by screaming chainsaws at any minute – as it had every day for weeks now.

Eventually she wandered out to her veranda. The Kincade Construction ship sat out on the horizon. It would be practically deserted now, with most of the men here on the island. She walked around to the back of her bungalow, and stopped dead in her tracks. The plantation had gone.

She could see the distant mountains, rugged and magnificent against a perfect azure sky. But their beauty was lost on her.

She stood. For what seemed an eternity, she stood and stared.

'Shannon! Shannon are you alright?'

She didn't respond to Dane's voice. She couldn't speak. All she could do was stand there and stare at the vast open space which once rang with laughter and bursts of song as copra workers got on with their work. Where parrots screeched and provided vivid bursts of colour amongst the greens and browns of the palm trees.

Then Dane was standing in front of her. 'Shannon,' he murmured softly. 'Didn't you realise we were this far on?'

She shook her head, her whole body numb.

'I assumed you were watching... Here let me take you inside. You're in shock.' His hand touched hers.

It felt like fire. 'Don't you touch me!' She saw him stiffen, saw his eyes crease as if someone had just sent a knife through his heart. She tore into him, hating him ... loving him. 'Are you satisfied? Now are you happy?'

'No, I'm not happy, Shannon. I would give anything to change things.'

'Stop saying that!' she cried. 'You wouldn't give anything at all! You haven't changed your plans one jot. You came determined to flatten our plantation and you've done just that. You've wrecked our lives, my grandparents have gone. I have nothing left...'

'Nothing?' he exclaimed, suddenly angry. 'Just how selfish are you?'

She stopped her rant.

'I beg your pardon?'

He shook his head and looked at her with an unusual harshness in his deep blue eyes.

'I understand your feelings. I know there's nothing I can say or do to make you understand that I didn't treat you unfairly. But sad though it is, the world does not revolve around you.'

She gasped.

He went on, white lipped. 'This airfield will bring employment to this island. People will be able to earn a decent wage, be able to afford a nice home, the economy growth will provide better facilities for the island. Where's your nearest hospital, Shannon?'

She hesitated, grasping the point he was making. 'Well, it's over on the next island.'

'And schools?'

'Yes! We have schools,' she answered angrily.

'How about colleges?' Her silence urged him to continue. 'No, the young people have to leave the island if they want to train for another profession.' She stood there, saying nothing.

His expression softened. 'I know all this is hurting you at the moment. But the sacrifice your family have made is something to be proud of.'

His words were beginning to make her feel small and selfish, and ashamed. Which no doubt was his intention. 'So, I should be celebrating, should I? Waving the flags and singing?'

He gave a small smile. 'No. I'm not asking that. I'm asking you to come to terms with these changes.'

She glared at him. 'If and when I accept these changes it will be on my terms, not because you tell me to.'

'Okay,' he agreed, hesitating then. 'But there's something else.'

She looked at him, her heart giving a strange little lurch. The way he was gazing at her, it was as if ... as if he did really care about her. 'Yes?' she murmured, hoping against hope that he was going to say the words that would unlock the mental barrier she had erected around herself.

He took a deep breath.

She saw the rise and fall of his chest as he

struggled with his words. 'Shannon, you have got to be out of your house by the end of the week. It won't take my men long now to get the runway laid. There could be a light aircraft landing with some government officials on board very soon and...' She didn't hear what else he had to say. She turned and stormed away, before he saw the damage he had done.

From her kitchen window, Shannon watched the progress of the airstrip being constructed. Dane Kincade's men were hard workers, she had to give them that. No doubt they were working to a time schedule and she was under no misapprehension that the first aeroplane would be flying in before too long. And gauging by the direction of the runway, her bungalow – and her – were major obstacles in the way.

Towards the end of the week she had a visit by two of Dane's men. She had seen them around but never spoken to either. Now they stood on her veranda in their hard hats and high-vis jackets.

'Yes?'

'Good morning,' the taller one said. 'Mr Kincade wants us to check that this house is now empty and ready for demolition.'

She smiled sweetly and opened the door to them. As they walked in, she swept her arm around the living room, indicating all her furnishings in place, the pictures on the walls, the vases of flowers on the window-sills.

'Gentlemen, I think you'd better tell your Mr Kincade that this bungalow is certainly not empty and definitely not ready for demolition.'

They looked at each other, blank confusion etched across their suntanned faces.

'I'm sorry miss, but it has to come down.'

'I think you'd better tell Mr Kincade that he'll have to change his plans.'

As they left Shannon felt the bittersweet taste of revenge. Dane was not having this all his own way.

Later that day when someone else knocked on her door, Shannon braced herself for a battle with Dane. To her surprise it was Denny and Corey standing there.

'Oh! Hi! Come on in guys,' she said.

Denny gave her a long searching look. Shannon turned aside, guessing he had noticed the dark circles under her eyes from the long sleepless nights of late.

'Shan, babe, this ain't on,' Denny said, standing in the centre of her room. 'You gotta move out babe. I'm sick with worry over you.'

'Me too,' Corey said, threading his arm through Shannon's.

'There's a plane due in the day after to-morrow,' Denny stated. 'It's gonna be sweeping low over the horizon, an' coming in across the bay. Straight this way babe. Wheels down, propellers whizzin', engines screamin'. It's gonna miss this rooftop by inches.'

Corey hugged her fiercely. 'I don't want you getting killed Shan.'

Her heart lurched and she hugged Corey to her. 'That won't happen Corey. They simply can't land if there's an obstacle in the way.'

'No, and it can't take off neither,' Denny said despondently. 'Which means that me and the other plantation workers ain't gonna be able to fly to Fiji to do the training courses that Dane's set up for us.'

'What?'

'We're due to fly out on the return flight. We've all got places on aviation and business courses. Dane wangled them for us. He's footing the bill too.'

'Is he?' Shannon breathed, realising suddenly this stand she was making was affecting more people than just Dane Kincade. 'How many of you are going off for training?'

'Twelve of us,' he answered, reeling off the names.

She sank into a chair, head in her hands, knowing the time had come to give in gracefully. She had to move out. Had to let them complete the airstrip and allow the planes to land, and progress all over the island to begin.

Corey was standing beside her, and she reached for his hands. 'Corey, will you find some big cardboard boxes and help me pack my things?'

His smile spread right across his face. 'You betcha!'

By early evening, her bungalow was an empty shell. As fast as she packed things up, one of the locals had whisked it away to her new home along the coast. She hadn't seen her new home for herself yet, and she was amazed to feel a tingling of excitement in the pit of her stomach at the prospect of making a new start.

'Shall we walk you down there Shan?' Denny asked as they stood looking around the empty bungalow.

Shannon kissed his cheek and Corey's too. 'No. I'll make my own way in a little while. I just want to spend a little time here, to say goodbye. Thank you both.'

'No worries Shan babe,' said Denny. 'Now you get your pretty face smilin' again. You ain't been yourself for a while now.'

She didn't argue. Didn't attempt to deny it. She just kissed them both, and waved goodbye as they headed home.

Shannon went back indoors. The sun was setting now, a brilliantly glowing orange ball bobbing on the horizon, colouring large areas of the ocean the deepest red.

She stood at what had been her bedroom window, gazing at the view. At least he couldn't take that from her – the beauty of the island. She would still be able to swim and dive for pearls. She could make jewellery from her new home as easily as from here.

With the dazzle of the sunset, Shannon didn't see the speck in the distance at first. Her mind was elsewhere, trying to work out whether Dane had deliberately tricked her as she believed, or whether, as he'd continually declared, his intentions had been well meaning.

If that was the case...

But then something caught her eye. Something directly in her line of vision. A speck of light in the distance. She frowned, trying to work out what it was. It was certainly growing larger, closer. And then she realised. An aeroplane was coming in low and straight for the island, heading for the barely completed runway – and her.

CHAPTER NINE

Shannon stood riveted to the spot. Like a rabbit caught in the glare of a car's head-lamps, she stood watching the aircraft coming closer. Now it was just skimming the waves, she could see the swirls of propellers, see into the cockpit window. Thought she could even see the look of panic on the pilot's face as he saw her bungalow in its path.

Its wheels were down, its engines screamed, and a black shadow engulfed her. The walls shook and rattled as if the whole place was caving in as the aircraft skimmed over her roof. She didn't remember throwing herself to the floor, but that was where she found herself as the deafening roar of engines passed overhead. There was a thud which shook the floor and reverberated through her body as the plane touched down and then came an even louder roar as it employed its reverse engines to stop on the limited stretch of runway.

Arms wrapped protectively over her head,

Shannon prayed that the workforce had known about this unexpected arrival, and that no one had been working in the vicinity.

Dane! Had he known about this? What had he said the other day about some government personnel flying into inspect everything? She tried to think … and then she started to feel sick. Sick to the very soul. He must have seen that she was finally moving out by the comings and goings of the constant stream of helpers. But he hadn't come and checked on her to make sure she wasn't still here.

He hadn't bothered to warn her that an aeroplane was due to land. She could have been killed.

Racked with misery she stumbled to her feet, trembling from head to foot, wanting to find him and tell him to his face how much she hated him.

Then everything seemed to drain out of her. What was the point in that? He didn't care if she lived or died. And so instead, she slumped down into a corner, too numb to even cry.

When the door was wrenched open a minute later, Shannon instinctively covered her head with her arms again, thinking something was falling in on her, some beam shaken loose by the vibrations of the plane. But it was just her door – and Dane standing there in the opening, looking frantic.

And then his eyes settled on her.

'Oh my God! Shannon! Dear God, are you alright? Are you hurt?' He was on his knees, cradling her, his eyes searching her face. He looked grey, Shannon thought, then wondered if it was just the strange light in here.

She looked at him. She wasn't shaking now, she felt oddly calm, devoid of all emotion. When she spoke her voice was flat. 'Tell me something Dane. Did you forget I might still be here or didn't you care whether I was or not?'

'What?' he gasped. 'What?'

'If I was out of your way, it would make life so much easier for you.'

His eyes narrowed, disbelief clouding his face. 'Why are you saying this?'

'I just want to know,' she said, looking directly into his eyes, a thought somewhere at the back of her mind wishing vaguely that the pain and anguish she saw in his face was because he loved her. But of course she knew that wasn't the case.

Still crouched down beside her, he ran his fingers raggedly through his hair. 'How could I forget about you and the precarious situation for a second? Shannon I didn't know that plane was coming in. Clearly someone in my higher management team took the call, and gave the all clear for landing. The first I knew about it was when I saw it approaching.'

'And I thought you were the boss,' she murmured flippantly.

'It's unforgivable,' he said, taking her hands and pressing them to his lips. 'Shannon, you honestly think that I would put your life at risk?'

'Yes,' she nodded, ridiculously finding a smile.

As she heard the words coming out of her mouth she knew this was all starting to become too surreal.

She gazed blankly around at the empty shell that had once been her home, even saw herself slumped pathetically in a corner. And this man, kneeling beside her whom she loved so desperately and who might be telling the truth, or might be lying. She knew then that she was in no condition to make judgements.

Very calmly she said; 'Dane, would you help me to my feet. I'm feeling a bit wobbly.'

Wordlessly, he eased her from her slumped

position, one arm around her waist, the other clasping her hand.

'I think I could do with a strong cup of tea now,' she said shakily, then suddenly burst out laughing. 'Oh! No I can't, can I? I've got no kettle, no tea pot, no nothing.'

And then her world turned black and she felt herself falling.

When Shannon opened her eyes again, she was in Dane's arms and he was carrying her along the beach. The sky was blood red now and she could hear the ocean singing to her. She closed her eyes and rested her cheek against his chest.

The bed he finally placed her in was her own, and confusion set in again.

'Where am I?'

'You're home Shannon. Your new home. You need to rest.' And Dane tucked the sheets around her neck and pressed his lips against her temple.

She wanted to reach out to him. To tell him not to go. But he was already at the door.

'Don't leave me,' she murmured. But her voice was so soft he didn't hear her. The door closed with barely a sound.

She awoke to the feel of warm sunshine on

her face. She opened her eyes, wondering for a moment where she was. And then the events of the previous night came flooding back to her. She lay there, re-living everything in all its horror. She had a vague memory that Dane had brought her here. She remembered his kiss.

There was a sound then. Someone was moving about in another room. She heard the distinct sounds of a teacup being stirred.

'Dane?' she whispered, her heart soaring as she clambered out of bed, finding she was still in yesterday's clothes. She peeped around the bedroom door, not recognising the layout of the house at all and finding herself in a corridor. She had to explore the various rooms until she found the kitchen. It was a beautiful kitchen, but the man standing there making breakfast, sent her hopes disintegrating into smithereens.

'Hey, Shan, babe! You okay girl? Man, what a night. That plane comin' in all unexpected. What a panic!'

'Denny! What are you doing here?'

'Just fixing you some breakfast. Poached eggs on toast an' coffee.'

'That's really kind, but you don't have to. I'm not ill.'

'You were in shock girl, an' I reckon you

were pretty exhausted, what with all that's been going on these last few weeks.'

'Maybe,' she agreed, sitting down at the kitchen table, looking around at the new cupboards. She couldn't have designed it better herself.

Denny placed her breakfast in front of her, pulled up a chair opposite and sipped his coffee. 'Dive in then girl. You need to build your strength up. You ain't been yourself at all recently.'

She found a smile. 'This is delicious, and so kind of you.'

'That's what friends are for.'

She ate, and the events of the previous night came back more clearly – in particular, the reasons Dane gave for not warning her about the aircraft.

'That plane was a bit of a surprise to everyone, wasn't it?' she ventured.

'Man! Wasn't it just. Folk are gonna have to buck their ideas up when we've got regular flights in and out.'

'So ... so who knew about it, do you think?'

Denny shrugged. 'Well, you've got to guess that the boss man knew...'

Shannon's eyes fluttered shut. So Dane had been lying – again.

Then Denny continued. 'Although from

what I heard, he went mental as the plane was comin' in. Went charging straight down the runway, straight down the beach. Folk are saying he looked like he was trying to stop that plane with his bare hands.'

Shannon raised her eyes. 'Did you see that?'

'Nah, me and Corey were halfway home. But it's what folk are saying this morning ... anyway girl, I gotta go. Gotta get packed. Seems we're flying out on that ol' plane this afternoon to start our training courses. Things have been brought forward.'

Shannon stood and hugged him and wished him luck, an image in her head that hadn't been there a moment ago. Dane running at the plane as if he were trying to stop it with his bare hands.

When Denny had gone, and she'd washed up her breakfast things in her new shiny sink, Shannon found her bathroom and discovered how her new shower worked, the image still in her head. Every room was more spacious than her old place. This was big enough for a family, and she hoped suddenly that she wasn't in the wrong bungalow.

Trying to get her thoughts in order, she spent the morning unpacking her ornaments and arranging everything to her liking. Could Dane really have put his own life in jeopardy to save her? Their conversation as she'd sat stunned in the corner of her old house was vague. She'd asked him, she remembered asking him. She barely remembered what his reply was though.

Shannon finally ventured out into the afternoon's heat, feeling refreshed and relaxed and more hopeful. Hope, she realised was something that had been missing from her life for quite some time. It was wonderful to feel it back again.

Looking around she saw that Dane had been right about the view and the breathtaking scents from the tropical flowers. It was lush here, deeply tropical. She would be able to create an abundant vegetable garden.

She'd been half expecting – and hoping – that Dane would call round and see how she was. After all that had gone on yesterday, her weeks of anguish over him seemed to have melted into insignificance. If his reaction last night was true, surely that meant he really did care about her.

She could still feel the strength of his powerful body as he'd carried her along the beach and the tenderness as he'd tucked her safely into bed, and kissed her.

Those weren't the actions of a man who didn't care about her. They were almost like the actions of a man who loved her...

She suddenly felt desperate to see him, to run to him and tell him how sorry she was for not realising he had been telling the truth all along. For not holding him that day when he had been so close to tears.

She set off towards the airstrip, walking briskly, feeling crazily, madly happy. Taking off her sandals, she splashed through the shallows. It dawned on her that it had been weeks since she's been swimming or gone diving. Suddenly, she wanted to get back to that. But first, she had to see Dane.

Skirting around the mass of green army style tents where Dane's men had set up camp she looked to see if he was there. There was no sign of him and so she asked the man nearest to her.

'I'm looking for Dane, do you know where he is please?'

The man glanced at his watch. 'Probably on board by now.'

'Sorry? On board? I don't understand.'

'The plane. He's heading over to Fiji.'

A sick sensation washed over her. She tried to quell it, tried not to panic. 'W ... why is he going there? Oh, it'll be to settle in the people who are going on the training course, I imagine.'

The man pulled a face. 'No, I don't think so. Hang on, he left our foreman, Mark in charge.' He shouted over to an older man who Shannon had seen around over the weeks. He came over and smiled.

'Hello there, how can I help?'

'Young lady was asking about the boss. He's heading back to Australia, isn't he?'

Shannon felt her knees buckle.

'Yes that's right. We had an early morning meeting and he explained the change of plans. Seems he's got two or three new contracts in the pipeline. Needs to head off and start negotiations.'

'How long will he be gone?' she asked bleakly.

The foreman gave her an odd look. 'Well that's it for him here. He won't be back. Worst part's over, we can get on with all the building work now, then we'll catch up with him wherever our next job is.'

'He's not coming back?' she choked, her heart breaking.

'No, no he won't.' He looked suddenly pityingly at her. 'If you need to see him you might still catch him. Plane hasn't taken off yet.'

She was already running.

'You'll have to be quick though, miss, they are leaving any minute now.'

She raced across the sand, losing her sandals at some point, her hair flying and her leg muscles pushed to the limits. She could hear aircraft engines starting up. 'No, please God no...'

In the distance she saw the plane, it was taxiing along the runway, its propellers whirling faster and faster until they became invisible. She forced herself on, running as fast as she could. But the plane was building up speed, building up to its crescendo of power, and then it moved forward, gathering momentum, powering along the runway and then lifting itself up from the tarmac. Her bungalow was gone. The workforce had made short work of demolishing it. The plane swept over where it had stood and rose higher into the sky. She thought she glimpsed Dane at a window.

Did he see her standing there, tears streaming down her cheeks? Did he see her collapsing into the sand?

She would look like a dot now, the plane was high in the pale blue sky, fast becoming a shining speck in the distance, and then it was gone.

'Oh, Dane,' she sobbed, her tears turning the golden sand into mud. 'Don't leave me ... please don't leave me. I love you!'

'And I love you, Shannon.'

On her knees, she thought she was hearing things. Thought her mind was playing tricks on her. And then he was on his knees in the sand with her and she cried out his name so loud the whole island must have heard.

She flung her arms around him, knocking him backwards into the sand, her lips seeking his which he willingly gave.

His arms wrapped around her, holding her tightly to him, and then he rolled her over until she was beneath him and he was kissing her with all the love and passion that she could only have dreamed of.

When finally they breathed again, and she could speak even though it was mingled with a love-crazed laughter, Shannon said, 'They told me you'd left for good.'

'I nearly did my darling. I was on the aircraft steps when I realised I couldn't leave without trying one final time to make you believe that I care ... that I love you.' She went to speak but he silenced her with another kiss. 'Last night when you thought I'd risked your life was the most hurtful thing. If you believed that of me, I felt there was no hope for us.'

'But you kissed me.'

'It was a kiss goodbye Shannon. You were breaking my heart. I had to get away before you destroyed me completely.'

'I didn't know,' she breathed. 'I was too wrapped up in my own misery. I'm sorry for not taking your word – for believing what Banners said instead.'

He raised an eyebrow. 'Yes well, he's no longer part of my team. He's actually on that plane and will be looking for a new job when he lands.'

'You've fired him?'

'It was Banners who gave the all clear for that aircraft to land last night. That's un-forgivable.'

Shannon gasped. 'He must really have disliked me, but why?'

'Probably because of the way you sent him packing last time. As for last night, we'll give him the benefit of the doubt. It might have been a simple case of human error – but one I can't afford to have around me. I shan't miss him Shannon But you...' and his eyes sparkled as his lips found hers again 'I would miss you terribly if you weren't in my life. Miss you unbearably.'

'Oh Dane, I love you so much. But what

about the new contracts you were supposed to be heading off to see?'

He smiled. 'I'll take another flight – one where you'll be coming with me. And how about when we stop off at Fiji we catch up with your grandparents and give them our news?'

'Yes, yes, yes!' she exclaimed joyfully.

'And when we finally get back here to this tropical paradise, we think about a beach wedding? You may have noticed young lady, that when I designed your new bungalow – in the vague hope of winning you round one day, I built it big enough for the both of us ... and maybe even one or two little ones eventually?'

Shannon searched for the words to convey her joy, but there were none that said what she wanted to say. And so she simply kissed him again and again – and again.

This Large Print Book, for people
who cannot read normal print,
is published under the auspices of

THE ULVERSCROFT FOUNDATION